Rus
Rushfield, Richard.
On spec : a novel of
    young Hollywood $ 21.95
1st ed.

W9-CNH-306

On Spec

A Novel of Young Hollywood

On Spec

A Novel of Young Hollywood

Richard Rushfield

ST. MARTIN'S PRESS 🐾 NEW YORK

ON SPEC: A NOVEL OF YOUNG HOLLYWOOD. Copyright
© 2000 by Richard Rushfield. All rights reserved.
Printed in the United States of America. No part of
this book may be used or reproduced in any manner
whatsoever without written permission except in the
case of brief quotations embodied in critical articles
or reviews. For information, address St. Martin's
Press, 175 Fifth Avenue, New York, N.Y. 10010.

Library of Congress Cataloging-in-Publication Data

Rushfield, Richard.
    On spec : a novel of young Hollywood / by
Richard Rushfield—1st ed.
      p.   cm.
    ISBN 0-312-24226-3
    1. Motion picture industry—California—Los
Angeles—Fiction. 2. Hollywood (Los Angeles,
Calif.)—Fiction. 3. Los Angeles (Calif.)—Fiction.
I. Title.

PS3568.U7273O6 2000
813'.54—dc21   99–054821

First Edition: March 2000

10 9 8 7 6 5 4 3 2 1

For Len and KR

Acknowledgments

Humongous thanks and appreciation to the following people. Every writer should have them all: my agents, Alex Smithline and David Vigliano, and my editor, Joe Veltre, for believing in the book through it all; my early readers/hand-holders Will Baum, Sean MacCaully, Jenny Konner, Mark Gerald, Lisa Derrick, Mark Ebner, Nicole Coady, and Peter Karlin; and my sister, Ali. Without you, I am a quivering bowl of Jell-O.

One

STU BLUMINVITZ
The Writer

Dateline: Hollywood.
No, no. That's wrong.
Dateline: Bluminvitz.
That's it. That has a nice ring.
Dateline: Bluminvitz.

Kyle says that no spec written on a laptop has ever sold, but I saw no less than Chris McQuarrie, author of *The Usual Suspects*, working on one at Stir Crazy last week. If Bukowski had had the technology, he would have used it.

I'm still looking for a buyer for *Kennel Break*, my Tarantino meets *Turner and Hooch* spec about two small-time hoods trying to break Scooby, their girlfriend's Rottweiller, out of the pound. My framing device gives the hoods the chance to get to know each other and hook up with some pretty weird characters while staking out the pound. I think my scene where they bury the night watchman while drinking Yoo-Hoos and rattling off their favorite *Starsky and Hutch* episodes really underlined the absurdity of American culture and the small value it places on human life. But at the same time it is an homage, not a mockery. I am trying to take a reverential approach toward kitsch.

Unfortunately, trying to do something different and make a statement doesn't always guarantee you an immediate payoff in Hollywood. My friend Josh, who works in the Praxaline Productions mailroom, slipped me a copy of the coverage they did on it. In the comments summary, the reader wrote, "A vapid, third-generation *Reservoir Dogs* rip-off drowns beneath its tedious one-note characters and incomprehensible *Die Hard* in a kennel story line." What do these readers know, anyway? I have faith that somewhere in this town at least one person will get the serious commentary I am making.

I have been hanging out with this really cool guy called the Pit Bull. He was a huge screenwriter back in the fifties (he did a rewrite on *Touch of Evil*, he says) but he burned out when the studios went corporate in the eighties. Now he spends most of his time hanging out at the Dresden drinking gin martinis. He really loves what I am doing and has given me tons of direction. He says I've got to stab Hollywood in the jugular and suck out its brains and that is what I am trying to do.

Despite the nasty coverage, things are beginning to turn around for me. Yesterday, I was at Eat a Pita, this falafel patio where I lunch when I'm sick of the Gumbo Pot. A stranger sat down to share the table with me and he turned out to be Eric Whitfield, one of Hollywood's hottest up-and-coming young producers, or so he told me. Over lunch, he asked me what I was working on and I told him about *Kennel Break* and he said it was exactly the kind of project he's been looking for. Small-time hood pics were his "numero uno" genre, he said. I am taking a meeting with him tomorrow night to pitch it.

On top of that, I finally met a really cool girl. Last night I was hanging out at the Formosa, this cool old forties Chinese bar, with the Pit Bull. As we were leaving, a beautiful blonde spilled her drink on me. I offered to buy her a new one and made a joke about how I used to drop my ice cream cones at Baskin-Robbins to get a new scoop for free. Instantly I could tell that we connected, not just on some Hollywood "let's do lunch" bullshit level, but as human beings. She let me buy her about eight more lemon Stolis and said she thought *Kennel Break* sounded hot. Her name is Chelsea and she is an actress. At the end of the night, she even gave me her number. I left a few messages today, but she must be out. I think Chelsea is the one I've been waiting for!

Oh, shit. My mother is yelling for me. All day she has been after me to clean up my room. When I sell this script, I am *definitely* getting my own place.

DEANA COHEN
The D-Girl

Okay, you guys. Can I just tell you, I have had the day from hell, do you know what I mean? First of all, my alarm clock goes off like fifteen minutes late; I've got to get that fixed. That means I'm running so behind at the gym I have to cut short my time on the Stairmaster, which sucks because last night after the screening at the Beverly Center, I went bonkers and ate like six Cinnabons with frosting. I can't believe I did that but I was so stressed there was literally no choice. Okay, then I'm on the Stairmaster and this towel boy is walking by totally scoping me out. I mean great, like I pay ninety dollars a month to get checked out by the towel boy when I'm all sweaty and gross.

So he's so busy ogling me that he knocks into my machine and the script I'm reading falls off the rack and gets stuck in the stairs. So I'm like, "Hello! Look out, you freak!"

And he says he's sorry but he recognized me because he was going to direct this Jackie Chan type action-comedy project that I was trying to set up last year but got put into turnaround because Jerry, my boss's boss, hated the title.

So I'm like, "Just get the script back together or it will be your ass if we miss out on this project, you loser."

But then he can't fish a few of the pages out of the Stairmaster and it's a spec and I have to give my boss a report by 9:00 A.M. So what can I do but just tell him it's a pass? I change the title page and give him the coverage of a script I read last week. He never looks at the reports anyway, do you know what I mean?

Then I take a meeting with this lame-ass writer about the rewrite of his script that he gave us a two-year option on. I totally want to go to Jerry with the project but we're on like the ninety-seventh draft and he still can't get it right. Can I tell you, I gave him all these notes last month and he totally did them like dead-on. So I told him that when I said I wanted the bus driver in scene fourteen to be older I meant like, Harrison Ford older, not Obi-Wan Kenobi. I mean, God! If he's going to do the notes exactly like I tell him and not even think about it I could just write the script myself.

So he starts like crying and saying he can't take it and he's broke or something. And I'm like, maybe you should be in a different business if you can't take the heat. God, men in this town are literally the biggest bunch of babies I have ever met in my life.

Speaking of which, I'm supposed to go on a date with Todd from the Neutron Agency tonight. He is so cute but I totally need to focus on my career and not be in a relationship now. It will still be cool though 'cause he'll buy me dinner at Matsuhisa and if I let him think I might sleep with him he'll probably let me read the spec by Rick Drain that he's going out with next week.

I think this nightly development-support group conference call is such a great idea. Kayla, you are genius for setting this up. People in our business, especially women, get so overlooked. It is great to have a place to share with people who truly understand. I'm literally dying to hear what you guys have going on, but I'm so late now that I have to hang up this second.

But before I go, can I just tell you guys, if I don't go in for a massage and a pedicure soon, I will lose it, do you know what I mean?

TODD HIRTLEY
The Agent

THE NEUTRON AGENCY
Memo: #14456
Agent: Todd Hirtley
Date: February 28, 1997

Write this down.
Write it.
Yes, slave, everything. This is your job. Do you want to keep your job? Then write, turd boy, now. Turd boy.
Paragraph. Where was my smoothie this morning? No, my Jamba Juice boysenberry-mango smoothie with protein boost. This is not a Jamba smoothie. This is shit. Are you getting this down? Because I am going to check every word, turdler. One spelling error and it's no company Christmas party for you.
Paragraph. The new Palm Pilots are here but I didn't get one. Did Marty's assistant order me one? It's a fuckup, no cause for alarm, right? Does Marty know I don't have it? Find out. Quietly.
Paragraph. That cheese-breath writer has been stalking me in the lobby. He is not to enter this building again. What was that script he tried to slip me? *Kennel Break*? A dog heist for

fuck's sake. He's banned from the building. Forever. Call security and tell them I want to set up a permanent ban. Persona non grata. In perpetuity. Tell Yvonne what's-her-name at reception. He calls, I'm out. When he calls back ask him what he wants. Wait two hours, call him back. Whatever it is, we can't help.

Paragraph. Conner from *Variety* is coming by this afternoon to do a piece on the young partners. Me and the boys. Did you see the Calendar section on Sunday? They're calling us the Wolf Pack now. The hottest sextet of up-and-comers Hollywood has ever seen. And now our party-boy agenting juggernaut is on the brink of ascending to the throne of this, the largest talent agency in the world. Find out what the others are wearing for the meeting. I want to look distinctive, stand out above the pack. Show the world that while the team is rising to the leadership of the agency, Todd Hirtley is rising to the leadership of the team.

Paragraph. Let's roll some calls. Jerry's nephew. Then try Jerry again. Schedule a lunch. Morton's. No, Cicaida. Closed? It did? Okay, Morton's. Call that development slut Deana Cohen. Supposed to dinner with her tonight. Tell her she's coming with me to the premiere of the new Michael Bay western. Meet her at the parking lot down the block. Half hour before screen time. Be nice. I'm sending her Drain's script next week. A slam dunk. I predict Drain's highest purchase price ever. Here's the sell: the pioneer of the slick-talking action comedy takes you inside the mind of a serial killer who is stalking himself. Take the *Something About Mary* concept inside out, but play it straight. The spec can't miss as my juggernaut rolls onward.

Now lemme see the memo, ass-face.

P.S. Buy suede shoes.

CHELSEA STARLOT
The Actress

Wow. Fucking diary.

Fuck this.

My acting teacher, Morton Karmellian, says it's good to take a look at your day so you can use the shit that comes up in your performance.

Whatever.

Marion, one of my four roommates in that place on Harper, kept a diary. When she was in Cedar's detox, I read it. It was all about clothes, a catalogue of what she wore every day. How the clothes made her feel. How they made her look. Who she fucked wearing them and what happened to the clothes in the process. She kept recoordinating these outfits like she was going to find the perfect formula to get fucked and hired by the perfect guy.

That diary was the most heinous waste of a life I've ever seen. But when I took it to class and performed it as a monologue, Morton said I had made the most complete breakthrough to honesty that he'd ever seen. It all would have been cool if Courtney hadn't told Marion about my reading when she got out of the hospital. And that's what happened to that apartment.

Diaries are the lamest.

Anywaysssss, so let's take a look at me.

Well, for starters, I am completely screwed right now because even though I'm expecting enormous profits from my Staples ad—which plays a zillion times a day—my old commercial agent is in the Caribbean or something and I can't get my check or line up any new auditions until I get my reel back from her. She was really good with that shit. No one else at her office gets it. Dude, her assistants are all so on drugs I want to kill them. Anyway, by myself, I booked a phenomenal cigarette campaign for air in Korea. I used every technique known to man or woman but I got that fucking job from Ilene what's-her-face, the casting agent on every job I go out for. Cigarettes are a lotta fun. I don't care what anyone says.

The Sunset Plaza Coffee Bean is exactly what I need right now. I could sit here until I die slurping mocha blendeds and checking out all the hot musicians stopping by after sound checks on the Strip. Judy says she gets tons of work just from hanging here two hours a day, sitting at a table right by the sidewalk. Every producer in town spends their days here. Most of them are full of shit and never produced anything but I just met the nephew of Jerry, the studio guy. He asked me out for tomorrow night. Psyched. This could be major.

Got to get back to class soon. I totally dig Morton Karmellian but there is no way I am becoming a Scientologist. They say Travolta might be at the Celebrity Center workshop though. That's worth considering.

I'm getting sweaty. Met a nose-picker writer named Stew at Formosa last night. I had to listen for a year about some Lassie Alcatraz movie Stew says I'm perfect for. Whatever. Gotta find new reps. I'm not going to settle for any half-assed representation. I want it all and I've come too far to take *no* for an answer.

Those British guys are back. What are you looking at? They are that band Inertia. That singer is hot. I wanna take full and total credit for that band. I was going out with the guitar player when they got together and I swear the entire concept of the band was my idea. But I'll bet they didn't even put me on the list for their show tonight. People'll rip you off if you let them.

I am not a prostitute. I don't have a sugar daddy. I just have me. You have to work for it. Omigod, I'm getting a parking ticket.

Fucking bitch gave me a ticket.

ERIC WHITFIELD
The Producer

Note to self:
Read more. I know it sucks, bro, but got to fucking do it.
The classics. They are high-concept gold mines. That's why
they're classics. Look into the rights for the *Iliad*. It's one location. Everyone knows the name. Nobody knows what it's about.
Eric Whitfield presents *Iliad*. It's so big it doesn't even need the
the. Katzenberg's animated the Bible. Just genius. Try to get a
copy of that old Katzenberg memo. He was so right. Budgets are
out of control. Gotta go indie this year. Sundance was a fuck fest
for Bobby and Kent.

Pursue conversation with that writer Stu from Eat a Pita who
had puppy meets *Papillon* project. Could be large. Can I get a
treatment? Did he get my card? On card, instead of *producer*,
put *productions*. The producer part is de facto. Is ipso facto.
Study more Latin before *Iliad* pitch. Set up some meetings with
Todd at Neutron. I've got an in through his assistant. He's gonna
love it.

I got the game plan rigged to the seams. I get some writers to
hand me over their scripts, get them practically gratis because
stories are a dime a dozen here. Look for some real hard visual
stuff with explosions aplenty and lots o' prime parts for my *chici-
tas* to show what they got. Then, with the project under my belt,
I get the boys back home to invest. They're all suffering at their
brokerages, but earning bundles. I'm promising to introduce
them to the fine babes when they come visit the set. This town
is wired for a mover like me to make a splash.

That chick getting the parking ticket was at the *Friends* wrap
party. Chauncey? So fucking hot. Lock and load, pick and roll,
baby. Green jeep, oh yeah. Look her up in Academy pig book.

Ingenue section. Does she come here a lot? I should come here
a lot. There's acres of tail here. The iced blendeds draw the hotties all day long. A man who wants to get a leg up in the producing game could do well to spend some serious time on this patio,
scouting the talent. *El problemo* is it's thirty-five minutes from
my house. Got to move to Hollywood proper. Sunset Plaza area,
but definitely hills.

We're dialing, we're styling, we're growing large to charge.
Oh, yeah boy.

JERRY
Chairman, The Hotatsi Studios

Hello. . . . Helllloo. *Hello!* Cheryl! Cheryl! This thing is busted!
Who the hell picked this out! I want their asses—(*muffled voice
in background*)
  No! It's fucking busted! I talk into it and I can't hear a goddamn thing. . . . What? I know it's a Dictaphone and when I pay
for one of these I want to hear a fucking voice on the *other goddamn end* and if I don't by two o'clock there is going to be such
a world of shit around here—
  I just record? There's no one on the other end? What the—?
Just to record, huh? All right, all right. Fine, get back to work
before I find myself an assistant who doesn't spend the whole
day exercising her jaw.
  Okay. Record. Dr. Birnbaum says I got to talk to this thing
every day. Express my anger. Listen to it later. *Grrrr.* Stupid
worthless shrink. Paying him five hundred dollars, an hour to
tell me to listen to myself. Wouldn't be wasting my frigging time
with him in the first place if Jane wasn't threatening to divorce
me unless I deal with my god-fucking-damn hostility. And what's
more, she could have the divorce and take the pain-in-the-fuck-
ing-ass kids with her if I could just get the stock price of this

lousy studio to some reasonable pigshit level where I could cash in my options and afford a fourth ex. But since that blunder years ago, every time I try to leave my office, I'm dragging around this fucking albatross tied to my neck. Jerry, the man who passed on *Jurassic Park*. After all my years of service to the entertainment industry, that's all anyone thinks of me. And don't think it hasn't gotten back to the Japs. Oh no. They're just looking for another fuckup to give them the chance to take me down. And how the hell was I to know that anyone wanted to see dinosaurs? Back in the seventies, buddies of mine lost their shirts on the *One Million Years B.C.* sequel. Sunk everything into a caveman picture, never saw a dime. Well, for damn sure that's a mistake I don't make again. People want dinosaurs, they'll get 'em. If I could ever get this joint off its lousy butt and working again.

Anyway, hostility. There's not much to say. I'm feeling pretty good today. I'm in a cheerful mood, all and all. These pills Birnbaum gave me must be working. Life is good. Although it might be a hell of a lot better if I wasn't surrounded by a bunch of *no-talent bloodsucking parasites who do half the goddamn work of a pack of trained monkeys and cost me ten thousand times as much plus benefits. And the goddamn so-called talent you spend three un-fucking-believable years developing a project for and decide they want to tour with their fucking band and leave me with Keifer fucking Sutherland to try to open a one hundred-and-twenty-million-dollar budget with. Try explaining that to the Hotatsi Corporation while they're already complaining about the billions they've thrown down the toilet on this place. And then some schmuck kid agent Todd something or Ivy League pain in the ass calling me hanging outside my office trying to meet me about some God knows what. . . .*

Ohhhhh . . . but life is good. I am very happy today. *(voice in background)*

Wha? Mr. Morahitsu? On the phone now? Holy Christ on the cross. Does he know I'm here? Good, tell him I'm in the G-5. Phone's down. Can't be reached until tomorrow. Hurry, hurry. Christ. The Japs are looking for me. Gotta hide. *(tape ends)*

Two

DEANA

No. I mean it, guys. *This* was the day from hell. Not only was my car broken into last night and my CD player stolen *with my Liz Phair disk in it* (like some car thief from the 'hood is really going to listen to Liz Phair) but Ben from TriWorld, who competes with me for scripts because his company has a deal with our studio, found out that I dropped the giant-ant script into the Stairmaster, sent his assistant to the gym to pull out the pages. I'm not sure how he found out but that towel boy is so fired. Then Ben called up Rosen, the agent who submitted it to me, and showed him the crumpled-up pages, telling him that I passed without reading it. So Rosen called me up, all like *wigging out*, and said that from now on he'll submit to Ben instead of me and that I can kiss good-bye any thought of seeing the *Chutes and Ladders* script he is going out with next week—written by a client that *I set him up with in the first place.* That is the first and last time I do a favor for anyone in this town.

But, no, you guys, can I just tell you, it gets worse. I had that date with Todd from Neutron, and his assistant called and said we were going to the premiere of Michael Bay's new Old West thriller. (I passed on the script. Great concept, but the second act doesn't start until page fifty and the protagonists are completely underdeveloped.) The assistant told me to meet Todd in the parking lot down the block from the Bruin. And I'm like, *duhhh*, which parking lot? Weasel boy said he thinks it is the one behind the Hamlet. So I get there and the Hamlet is like, closed, gone, *fini*. So there I was stuck in traffic and I got on my cell and called up the assistant at the office and he called Todd in his car, who also couldn't find the Hamlet. So finally the assistant told us to just go to the lot behind where the Hamlet *used to be*. Why he couldn't have told us that in the first place is, like, a total mystery, do you know what I mean? Remind me to tell Todd that he has got to get a new assistant.

I met Todd in the lot and we walked over to the Bruin. Some event staff guy tried to make us go in on the side and not down the runway because, he said, our invites were the wrong color, which is total bullshit. We were there because of our connections. It's not like we won the tickets in some KROQ giveaway. Anyway, we hung out in the lobby and I pulled a pretty slick maneuver. Every time Todd started to talk to someone about Rick Drain's new script, I interrupted and asked him to go save seats for us, knowing that he had no intention of watching the movie. But he got nervous, thinking someone would find out that he was not staying, and forgot about the script. By the time he collected himself, whoever he was talking to was gone.

When the movie started we went to Hamlet Gardens for dinner. And then the greatest thing that can happen on a first date happens. In walk Tonya, Kayla, Deana, Lisa, Tonya, Michelle, Leslie, and Deana, who are all ditching the premiere too. I don't think anybody actually watches movies anymore. Todd got all bitchy when I told him we had to sit with them and sulked through the whole meal. (He is such a queen!) But it was cool to have a chance to see everyone. Tonya was just made VP at Verbatim and the other Tonya is going out with Jerry's nephew. Those guys are doing great! I really feel like I've blazed a trail for them, being the first of our generation in development to get on a desk of her own. I remember how harsh and defensive the women on desks were when I got here. I decided not to play that game at all. I'm going to be a mentor.

We got back for the end of the movie and told everyone how much we loved it. Even though I didn't see it, I could tell it was really well done. I would love to set something up with Bay. He has such a feel for that nineties hard-edged style with a spiritual twist.

We drove over to the party, which was rodeo themed, with big chuck wagons and clowns harassing you when you're trying to get food. It was way crowded and impossible to grab enough to eat and Todd bothered me all night to introduce him to Jerry. Finally, Jerry walked by and saw me and says "Goddamnit, stop standing around eating chicken wings. Find me a fucking project before I have to sell the whole studio for scrap metal." I totally respect the way he stays focused on work.

Todd introduced himself and drooled that he would really like to get together and talk about some scripts that would be perfect Hotatsi projects. Then, as Todd talked, Jerry started making this choking sound, like he was going into a seizure or something. Todd grabbed him from behind and tried to Heimlich him, but Jerry's throat cleared up and he screamed "Get away from me, you ivy-covered putzbag! Deana, get him away from me!" So I told Todd I had to go to bed soon because I have spinning class at 6:00 and we left.

While we were waiting for our cars at the valet, I ran into Tonya, Kayla, and Tonya again. Tonya was totally freaking out because Jerry's nephew was at the party with some model and when he saw her he said "Hi, Tina." So while I'm like dealing with her, it was an out-of-control crowd scene at the valet and I lost Todd. When my car came I called him in his. He asked if he could come over. "Todd," I told him, "I would totally love to hang out but I still have three scripts to read before I go to bed."

He gets all sulky, "This is your chance, Cohen. If you blow it, then . . ." The line started breaking up and I couldn't make out what he was trying to threaten me with but just then I remembered the Rick Drain script and told him to meet me at home.

He stopped by and we hung out a little bit and fooled around. I was beyond too tired for sex, though; do you know what I mean? Afterwards, we were like lying there and he says we should go out again and I said, "I'd love to get a look at the Drain spec."

"I'll think it over. At the moment, the situation is very fluid," he said. Then he left. You guys, can I just tell you, I hear Club Med in Aruba is having half-price next month. We have to go!

~~DATELINE: BLUMINVITZ~~
~~DATELINE 2000: BLUMINVITZ~~

DATELINE: BLUMINVITZ 2000

Yeah.

Hooray, I'm finally on my way. The big meeting came down and yours truly went over big. Way big. Okay breathe out, Stu, slow down, kid. Let me back up. I knew the whole night was off to an incredible start when I called Chelsea, who for the first time in a week was actually home. She sounded surprised to hear from me, but when I told her about *Kennel Break*'s prospects, and how I was meeting with Mr. Whitfield that night at Bud's, she agreed to maybe stop by and talk it over. I don't think she's stuck up at all, just shy.

Anyway, I stopped at my friend Friedbag's to borrow his suede half-coat for that urban terrorist-drugstore cowboy look, to show Whitfield that I'm not just some kid from the Valley with a curfew. I've lived! I rolled up to Bud's around 7:30 so I wouldn't have any hassle with the door personnel who I don't really know yet. Bud's is a really cool hangout for the young movers and shakers but its a little too "industry" for me to hang out at when I'm not there on business. I had awhile to wait so I ordered about four beers, and a chicken quesadilla. The beer was tasting good. I was nervous. I can admit it, it was my first real pitch in the majors, and I had a few.

While I waited, I saw sitting alone at the bar—this beautiful redhead in a leather miniskirt. She was really pretty, but no Chelsea. I could tell she was a real girl, not a Hollywood phony and figured she was probably feeling as out of place as I was, so I sauntered over to see if she was looking for company.

I grabbed the bar stool next to her and asked, "Is anyone sitting here?"

She shrugged and looked straight ahead, so I sat down.

"Your first time here too?" I tried for an icebreaker.

"Not," she said, snorting a little. "Who let you in?"

"Ummmm, I'm here for a meeting."

"What do you do?"

"I'm a writer."

"No kidding. Anything I've seen?"

"Not yet, but one year from now—"

She cut me off by waving over the bartender. When he came, she whispered something in his ear.

"You're sitting in her friend's seat," he told me, with a tone suggesting that my status at Bud's was not quite VIP.

"She said it was free."

"I guess she made a mistake, So you gonna move?"

There are times to stand your ground and times to run away. An hour before the biggest meeting of my life was definitely a time to run.

I strolled back to my little table and ordered another beer. Enough fooling around, I told myself, and used the rest of the wait to get focused.

Mr. Whitfield showed up around 10:00, forty-five minutes late, but he recognized me right away. I guess he had to check in with Bud first, which is cool because Bud got a good look at me. Next time I might not have to wait at the door if I come at a regular hour. Pretty soon, Mr. Whitfield returned with two Absolut Kurants—one for me—and suggested we move to a table near the back. He took a reserved card off the table and burned it with his lighter. Weird. But these power players will have their games. As we settled down to business, Mr. Whitfield told me about his incredible success streak, being involved—or close to being involved—with a major string of hits. He told me that he introduced the guy who did the CD-ROM for *Jingle All the Way* to the director's son and got producer's credit on the game. Right now he's working on a Dan Cortaj music trivia and action-game show he's set up, kind of a cross between *Jeopardy!* and ultimate fighting, he said.

At last, we came around to the script. I took my time setting the table like the Pit Bull said. I gave him my brief bio. English major at Reed, my stint as film reviewer for the *Eugene Trib*. Minor exaggeration, but who's counting? My incredible experience in Robert McKee's weekend screenwriting seminar; including how Bob pulled me aside during smoke break and asked if I was a lawyer. And how I'm pretty much full-time writing now, cranking out a hit machine.

I could tell he was eager to hear more about *Kennel* so I gave him my revised twenty-five or less: Tarantino meets *Turner and Hooch* about two small-time hoods (Think: Buscemi/Keitel) who've got to break their girlfriend's Rottweiller out of the pound, because only Scooby knows where he buried the loot. Whitfield's eyes lit up like a gremlin. Boom. I'd done it. The breakthrough meeting. It's all in how you deliver the moment. He could see the whole film from there. Before I could say "guild minimum," Whitfield was talking about going to his people at the studio.

At the studio! Hello drive-ons, good-bye tour bus! He took the script from me saying something about splitting the spec money over fifty thousand up between us, three quarters to him, so, duh, I took it and signed his papers. I suppose I should have looked them over but hey, he's taking me to a studio! That's when I saw this girl who looked just like Chelsea standing at the bar—what a night! I waved *come here* but I guess she didn't want to disturb our meeting because she turned away. No worries; I noticed she kept looking over at our table anyway. She would be so perfect to play goon number two's girlfriend. Mr. Whitfield wanted to take the script and "run with it." Just by the sounds of it he could tell "we got hugeness on our hands." For a moment I worried that the concept would get too Hollywoodized, but I guess anyone who sets up a Dan Cortaj project understands edgy.

We shook to seal the deal, and business behind us, I looked around for Chelsea. I musta been a second too late. Oh well, I was pretty tired. Anyway, I've got a feeling that now that she's seen me at work, I'll have her eating out of the palm of my hand. Mr. Whitfield picked up the check (for everything), which was classy but totally unnecessary—I was having the night of a lifetime!

We're off, Mom and Dad, your little boy's all growed up! (*Swingers*. Awesome movie. Vince Vaughn for *Kennel Break?* Ask Mr. Whitfield about availability.)

THE NEUTRON AGENCY
Memo: #14457

Are you getting this? I will ask you again, are you getting this? Remember, butt pirate, my every word is your gospel. Do not let one of them go unrecorded. Every golden word I speak will flow directly from my lips, onto your note pad, into the Power-Book, to be sorted, itemized, and placed in the proper file. Don't mess it up, turd boy.

First of all, get this down. I . . . *fucked . . . up*. *No!* Not I! Not your lord and master. I never fuck up. *You* fucked up. Write that. Your chance to crawl out of the slime pit has a date with the woman who is his in to one of the eight most powerful men in Hollywood. And what do you do? You set up their meeting him behind a restaurant that does not exist!

Yes, I know it only closed three days ago. But it is your job never to fall three days behind the curve. With a three-day lag, you might as well be dead. You must anticipate every possible variation of my needs and have them satisfied before they enter my head. So write it again: *I fucked up*. Okay. You are not fired, this time. Consider yourself on triple probation. Remember, shithead; Todd Hirtley is the only friend you have in this town and if you lose him . . . well, best not to even think of that possibility.

So after our little parking lot screwup, Deana and I finally met. Didn't look as bad as I remembered. She's lost some weight. Find out how. I want the name of her diet, her gym, her trainer, and her weight-loss counselor by noon today. *Go!*

Sit down. I am talking to you.

New paragraph. In the Bruin lobby, I preach the gospel of Rick Drain. I tell people it's already sold. Won't say to whom. Drive them crazy. This sale will be a cakewalk. Efforts interrupted, however, by Deana asking me to get her Junior Mints and a Diet Coke. I think she was planning to watch the movie. She is young yet, she will learn. When I was in the mail room, I used to watch the movie too. But then I learned that only losers watch covers. If you want to close the deal, you're not going to do it in a dark, silent auditorium. Remember: The lobby is where the closers stay.

After it starts we head to Hamlet Gardens to eat. Seven of what look to be Deana's OA support group are there. Deana insists we join them. She certainly knows how to show a date a good time, but at least it spared me from having to slog through a meal solo with her. Someone named Tonya has a date with Jerry's nephew. Look into it.

Got back to theater as movie is letting out. I run into Bay on the way over to the party. Had met him when Rick was pitching his *Garanimals* script. I tell Bay that I had never thought Hollywood could make a Western to top *Silverado* but he has proven me wrong. He said I should lunch with his assistant. Follow up on that.

At the party, cannot get lard-ass Deana away from the buffet line to introduce me to Jerry. Finally, he comes over to let her have it for leaving the office so early. And what do you know? God looks after his own. Just as we are introduced, Jerry chokes on a *taquito*. And whom but your master is on hand to execute the Heimlich I learned in summer-camp EMT course. Jerry is so moved by my rescue that he rushes off in tears. Remind me to send him a thank-you note.

At the valet line, I spot Jerry's nephew across the crowd. Deana is engrossed with her Save the Whales Committee, so I give her the slip and talk to him about watching the Mighty Ducks game together next week.

Get my car and call Deana in hers. The bitch is so ready for it that I can practically feel the heat through the satellite connection. Meet at her place where she has 2,000 scented candles lit in anticipation of my arrival. Give her ninety minutes of the Hirtley special and by the end of it she's begging to take Drain to studio. Tell her I'll get back to her and exit. The drumbeats grows louder by the moment.

Why are you still sitting there? I want this scanned and filed and I want my Jamba Juice! *Go!*

KILIMANJARO PRODUCTIONS
Eric Whitfield
Producer

Oh, yeah, I was feeling it last night, top of my game, triple double with an extra scoop on the side. My shit was freaky. Hit

Bud's around ten and the place was crawling. Got waved through the ropes by Gary who remembers me as the man who gets him the weekend big-dollar work at mansion parties. I *entrez* and saddle up to the bar. *Absolut rocks.* To my right, Bud was doing time with some mint model I woulda loved to enjoyed, but he aces her for a quick smoke with his homey. What a stud. Seriously, you don't get to be as dialed as Bud without knowing who every single dude in your bar is and what he's got to put on the board. This season. With knowledge comes skirt, and my man is rolling in it. A-list. The finies. He and I have been chatting about joining forces and starting an action-based production house together. Bringing together our extensive Rolodexes under one roof. My main man Faisal's got an in to Christopher Lambert who word has it has got three weeks free this summer and is shopping for a project. For now, though, I am stalling on the negotiations. I need to gather a little more juice to bring to the table and strengthen my side of the bargain.

I coulda headed with Bud to the VIP room for some of the real thing, but I was meeting the writer I discovered, Stu Blumkin-something. The poor squid was waiting for me at an egregious front table, where he stood out like a boob job gone bad. From the looks of it, he was well on his way to being pretty rocked. I gave Stu the nod, fired up two more Absolutes, and rolled over. "Whassup, Enrico Suave?" We moved to a reserved table Bud holds for his crew. I torched the "reserved" card with my lighter and watched Stu. He loved it.

But it was game time. I got totally focused. My mind went to rule three: The thing with writers is you never know. Tarantino was wanding videos in Redondo Beach. It's the world's hardest profession to gauge because it's the only one you can't judge by looks. Even the big-time seven-figure scribes look like schlumps who would never make it past any respectable velvet rope. Stu here was a dime-a-dozen desperation, but he'd written something and he was giving it to me. Why? Because I had an in on studios, and he couldn't use their bathrooms without permission. It's all about access, baby, and studio-wise, I am dialed. I could take him away from his nothing life and he knew it. The boy was basking in the sun. Stu'd never even gotten into a place like Bud's before. The mule had a string of duck quesadilla dripping from his lip, but, like I said, you never know.

I fed him another drink. What was in it for Kilimanjaro Prod? I just had a gut. Rule five: Gotta trust your gut. What Stu said before about this Lassie heist concept had a kind of Spader-Stoltz vibe to it that I could print money with. He handed me the script, too drunk or too scared to ask what his rights were. A good move on his part because he has none. It was mine now, jack. I flipped through. It was like vintage gangster-talk, man. Quentin all the way to the bank and that retro shit sells. I told Stu if the script's got any balls at all, we'll go wide. Here's the terms, he eats first, then I take seventy-five percent of all cash money over fifty K on the spec minus my expenses, bank the development seed money, and, hey, we're all friends in success, right? Stu nods unsurely. He's in. He's got no choice. It's me or back to the video store, right? We shake.

And that's when I spot her, that hottie from the Bean. I'm nearly positive she's been scoping me out. Last night I looked her up in the ingenues section of the SAG pig book. She's got a manager, a commercial agent, but no roles. She's giving me the go-ahead. With a pat on the back, I slide Stu my card, and bump my way to the bar. "Aren't you Chelsea Starlot?" She eats it up. We cruise back to VIP so I can introduce her to Bud. He woulda been so psyched but he was in the men's hoovering it with some model, so we cruise out the back.

I mean this chick is buying what I got to sell, big time. But I'm not taking her back to my place, no way. She's strictly hills. I am going to be locked into the groovin' pad soon but in the meantime I've been chillin' at this little five-hundred-and-fifty-dollar a month security building. Ya know, the generic white stuccoed hallways, waitress neighbors, and hyper-chlorinated, lukewarm overcrowded Jacuzzi. It's a happening scene for me now, can always make some time with one of the locals who lay out by the pool all day, but it is not in the ballpark of a major league Betty like Chelsea. So, I gave her the earthquake damage story and before you can say "titanic rack" we're rolling one car back to her place. Oh, yeah, I was in my zone, cruise control, lock and load, the Mac is back.

CHELSEA

Wait. No, seriously, wait. I'm on a roll here. My new stalker, Stupid might actually have a hot script. I was on with my commercial agent when call-waiting goes *click* so I think it's Tiana, who's supposed to be busy getting us on the list for Dragonfly tonight, so like a moron I take the call and *doinggh!* it's Stu Stalker calling for the 8,145th time that day. I will never give my home number to writers! I was so completely wrecked, I can't believe I did that. So, he goes he's got this meeting set up with a big producer at Bud's that night and do I wanna drop by.

"How big?"

"From what I hear, A-list," he says.

I go, "Maybe I'll show," and hang up. I was thinking he was full of shit and I hate Bud's. Bud is an ass-kissing creep, but Jerry's nephew said he hangs out there and I'm not walking away from any producers or even possible producers this month. August is all about saying yes to anything that might be something.

I tell Tiana that she's on her own tonight. She tries to talk me back into hitting Dragonfly by promising that this Iranian kid that she met last week, a junior at Beverly Hills High, will be there. I know that doesn't sound so hot but Tiana says this kid uses his parent's credit cards to buy, like, unlimited mountains of blow.

Actually, Tiana's plan did sound pretty fun but honey, I tell her, I needed a fucking job yesterday, so Dragonfly is out of the question tonight. That starts her on this whole guilt thing about how I'm always bailing on her and just using her now that I'm banned from my usual check-cashing place.

So I'm apologizing but all the while I know what this is really about. It's about Tiana's hot for the fucking bassist of the band that's playing tonight and knows that she is nowhere close to hot enough to get tagged to go back to their suite at the Mondrian. How-fucking-ever, one look at my latex-encased stilts and the doors fly open.

Anyway, fuck Tiana if that's what I'm good for. I told her that if she can't swim in Hollywood, she'll just have to sink like everyone else. The one-way bus ticket back where you came from, if you can afford it.

So I head over to Bud's, first stopping to score a half of not very good blow from the maître d' at La Imperial just a few doors down. I shouldn't have bothered because Eduardo's shit is so cut to the bone and does not go with my Vicaden prescription at all. I gotta find a new connection.

I cruise to Bud's at eleven, teeth gnashing like nuts. The line is enormous but Gary—who I did a Cheetos audition with—is working door and wants everyone to think he knows me so he waves me right in. "See ya, wouldn't wanna be ya," I say.

"Say that while you can," he spits out. "I got a callback from Nike today." Ouch, that hurt. I gotta admit, it did.

The lights are off inside and I can hardly see my way to the bar. Bud's is cool if you're too wasted to care, but otherwise forget it. There's not even one dance floor. And zero celebs. One guy who plays the best friend on a WB sitcom holds court in a corner booth, he's the biggest name in the house tonight. I go to the bar, get a Perrier—I've got to look for fucking work tomorrow—and scope for Stu. He is sitting with this guy, who looks to be about twenty-six, way too young to be a producer who actually produces. But he's got on a hot black Dolce & Gabbana suit with a lavender silk shirt unbuttoned halfway that he must have laid out a grand for. It's worth a closer look. I go to their end of the bar where I can hear everything and have to pretend not to see Stu, who is waving at me like a freak on meth.

The "producer" is sort of hot, sort of bald, but at least he's not eighty or anything. I can't believe Stu has a string of cheese hanging across his chin. What a dork! My own stalker, I'm so proud. The guy, who Stu keeps calling "Sir," says how the unit sales of Colonel Mustard, Don Cortaj's break out role, which he was somehow involved in, were enormous. Cortaj is Scientologist. I had him in Morton's workshop. Big, big fag, but that film was huge on video, or so I heard. This weasel is definitely not huge yet but something about the suit tells me he's not nobody. He could possibly get me into some feature callbacks, or at least TV. That's what these wannabe hotshots do; kiss up to the casting agents so they can pull strings for the girls they can use to impress the money guys. I couldn't believe he was with Stu, but I guess someone has to write the scripts.

I see the weasel staring at me, and point to the VIP room so I don't have to deal with Stu-pid. He tears his pants getting his money out and follows me inside. He knows my name, which is weird, but says he's not a Scientologist. In this industry you've got to be Scientologist or gay to get anywhere. Whitfield, that's his name, says he'll join if I wanted. I bet he would too. Now, I'm not sure any more if he's at all huge so I ask him, "What have you done that I would know about?"

Whitfield says he's got something set up at Zeus World, and that he's looking for the right director. Zeus World? Aren't they cartoons? Well, what the fuck, they're a studio, right! He stares at my saline implants that are paying themselves off already. He looks like a balding Andre Agassi on a very, very bad day. Goatees were in, then way out, and now they're in again if you didn't have one before. Eric's blows. I think that I might as well fuck him tonight.

Dear Jerry,

I wanted to take this opportunity to tell you how much I enjoyed our meeting at Bay's party last night. I am very grateful that I studied CPR so that I could have the opportunity of saving your life when you began choking. I am overjoyed to have been able to help someone whose work I admire and respect so deeply, a man whom I know is destined for nothing less than conquest of the entire industry!

Thank you again for allowing me to be there for you and if there is anything I can ever do for you, please do not hesitate to call.

> Wishing you huge grosses and
> enormous profit,
> Todd Hirtley
> The Neutron Agency

Three

THE NEUTRON AGENCY

Memo: #14458

This is a day that will long be written in infamy? No, no. This day will long live the infamy. How does that go, shit-for-brains? No. Not Roosevelt, Darth Vader. Find out. Get me the script, the shooting script, not the Barnes & Noble version.

Today your master stuns and baffles Hollywood with his death-defying display of agent superpower. Today we launch Rick Drain's hottest script yet. Copies made? Good. With the new red Neutron covers? Good. Double-sided pages? Show we are not wasting paper? Remember, Keith from Dunkirk is cohosting that rain forest benefit. Addressed? Good.

I want the fleet of messengers assembled here, ready to deploy by 9:00 A.M. Time their release so that every script hits its appointed desk exactly at 10:00 A.M. That means Valley runners leave here by 9:17 A.M. Except for Deana Cohen; promised her an early preview, so deploy to Hotatsi by 8:45 A.M.

I have worked the town into a frenzy. Yesterday, 9:00 A.M.— made three calls; dropped word that this script makes Drain's last two actioners look like *Romper Room*. Big thrills, I told them. Ten A.M.—word goes out that script has sold. Eleven: call my targeted readers—tell them this is not the script for them, it's all wrong for their companies. Have them begging for a look. One o'clock—let word fly that Clooney is on board, passing on *Batman VII* to make this—sight unseen! Two o'clock—the script is no longer viable. Three P.M.—spread the word that it is terrible. Drain's worst work yet. Out of date, clichéd. Going back for rewrite. Four—speed dial list and tell them, you can't have it! Five o'clock, I take my phone off the hook and go home.

Couldn't sleep with phone ringing all night, so I went over to Cohen's house and cut her a break. I am a man of extraordinary compassion, shit boy.

Okay it's 8:15 A.M. Why are you still sitting there, dumb shit? Assemble the messenger fleet, I want to make a speech. How's my hair? With the jacket or without? Without; I thought so. My master plan has taken shape beautifully. The buzz is all directed towards one Hotatsi Studio, which is so desperate for an A-list actioner—or any material, for that matter—that they will shit themselves when they learn I am giving them a stab at Drain. Then once Jerry and I are in bed together, it's no more dining D-girls for me. My list will begin at studio heads and go up from there.

Remember this moment. This is the closest thing to the big time you are ever going to see.

DEANA

Finally! All those weekends living like a shut-in with a stack of scripts, the late nights, the meetings with clueless writers, finally, it has all paid off! You guys, I might not have much time to talk in the future, because I'll bet dinner at Chaya that by this time next month I am going to be a VP! That's right, Todd gave me the Rick Drain script and it is in Jerry's hands as we speak.

So this is how it happened. I've been, like, noticing, that whenever Jerry's nephew is in the room Todd starts, like, you know, fixing his hair and acting all nervous like a teenage girl or something, do you know what I mean? So yesterday morning, Tonya tells me that Jerry's nephew finally rescheduled the date that he stood her up on and they were going out that night. So I tell her, after dinner, why don't we meet for drinks at Bud's before you go to SkyBar. Tonya was totally into that idea because she is so nervous that she won't have anything to talk about with him and she knows she can trust me—I would *never* steal a guy from one of my girlfriends. You guys are worth so much more to me than any guy ever!

So I call Todd's assistant (*such* a loser) and even though I know we don't have plans that night, because Todd is busy launching Drain's script, I leave a message saying I can't get together because I am meeting Jerry's nephew. Then I sit and wait by the phone and start counting. When I get to thirty-seven, *bingo!* There's Todd on the phone.

"I understand you are seeing Jerry's nephew tonight," he says.

"Oh, like, where did you hear that?" I play it cool.

"I have my sources," he tells me, totally deadpan.

"Todd," I say, "I would *sooo* love to talk to you, but you don't even understand how much work I have."

"Uh-huh. Just tell me one thing: What could you and Jerry's nephew possibly have to talk about?"

"Oh, my God. So much. I've got to fill him in on what everyone's up to. And you know he missed Sundance this year so I promised to tell him about all the parties. But Todd, I've got to go. You know Jerry has been freaking out about wanting to get a new script moving forward this week, and since I don't see anything on the horizon from your end, gotta work the phones. . . ."

"What about Drain's script? You don't think you would be interested in that?"

"I didn't know I was getting Rick's spec."

"I might be able to give it to you."

"You know what would be so great—if I could get it a day early so I can read it before I recommend it to Jerry."

"No can do. We launch tomorrow. The savages are beating down my doors. The town is white-hot hungry for Drain."

"What about tonight? You might give it to me over drinks?"

"Will Jerry's nephew be there?"

"Todd, he and I have got to talk. But, I suppose you might stop by. Can you bring the script?"

"Can't do it tonight. Have sworn to everyone, no copies leave the office before tomorrow. I will be crucified if I give you a day head start."

"How about six A.M. tomorrow? Send it to me first thing."

"I'll give you a fifteen-minute head start. It hits desks at ten A.M. You get it by nine-forty-five."

"Make it eight."

"I can do nine."

"Eight-thirty?"

"Deal. Where are you meeting?"

"Bud's. Ten o'clock."

"See you there."

We meet at Bud's. Tonya comes in with Jerry's nephew an hour late. She seemed really nervous because I don't think he's into her. I felt so bad; guys never are with her. She's just too available for guys for them to take her seriously as relationship material. When I introduce Jerry's nephew to Todd, they both acted like they had never met. Whatever! Anyway, he and Tonya only stay like fifteen minutes and after they leave, Todd gets all pissy and says he has to get to rest up for the big launch day.

This morning I woke up at 5:45, so I can get to the gym and make it to my desk by 8:00 to be ready for the script. The messenger came at 8:45. (Imagine that; an agent keeping his promise. That must be a world's first. But I did get the feeling that Todd is different than most agents.)

The script is amazing. I only had a chance to read the first ten pages before I took it up to Jerry's, but you get a nose for concept when you work in this business long enough, do you know what I mean? Rick Drain is the next Shane Black. I mean, his take on the serial-killer concept was just, like, amazing. The premise is that the killer is stalking himself. I've got a great head for premise and I know this one is hot. Rick so deserves all the money he gets.

I rushed the script up to Jerry's office. He is reading it right now and I told Todd to expect a bid before noon.

You guys, I might get really busy after this project gets moving and not have much time for you, but I want you all to remember that I totally support you, whatever you do. And I'll always remember how you were there for me when I was a nobody!

TO: ALL HOTATSI EMPLOYEES
FROM: JERRY
RE: WHY ARE YOU WASTING MY TIME

It has recently come to my attention that many of my employees confuse this studio with a charity institution. For this sorry state, I can only blame myself. After all, wasn't it me who has allowed everyone on this lot to live under the illusion they can collect paychecks at the end of every month without first going through the formality of putting in a single, honest day's work?

This confusion, while understandable, has recently grown to intolerable proportions. Thus, I am sending this friendly little reminder of why some of us bother to show up at work every morning.

You are employees of a movie studio. We are in the business of making movies. No. Scratch that. We are in the business of making money. We do not make money by wasting our boss's time burying him from head to toe in nitwit serial-killer scripts that have no ride and no toys.

I bring this to your attention because I had the opportunity to spend the entire morning reading—or trying to read—such a script, thanks to an urgent message from your coworker, Deana Cohen, telling me she had a "can't miss" project.

Let me clarify where I stand once again—when I say "rides and toys" I mean "rides and toys." A middle-aged detective chasing around a sociopathic bookworm is not a ride and is not a toy. Bring me rides and toys, now, before we sell every one of you into white slavery at our Jap owner's sweatshops. And animals. I want animals scripts, for godsakes. Jesus fuck the rest of you, do I have to do all your jobs myself?

Finally, in keeping with the vacation resort atmosphere we have established here, I have decided that this month's pay shall reflect that tone. July's paychecks for all staff will be cut by one-third. If anyone has any questions, please take them up with Miss Deana Cohen at ext. 2458. And if you still don't like it, *you can get off your lazy asses and get a real job pushing carts of overcoats down Ludlow like I did for half my life. Or sue me if you like and I'll have the legal department get off their butts to tear each and every one of you into a million little pieces.*

Thank you all for your attention and devotion. I look forward to working with you to churn out more Hotatsi magic in the next fiscal year.

KILIMANJARO PICTURES
Eric Whitfield
Chairman

Oh, freak yeah, had a little crisis but came outta the tunnel macked. That little hottie Chelsea, my go-to-girl, was asking to come up and see the hill house, "top of Nichols," the two-mil homes but cool, and I was diving on the thousandth excuse, when it hit me. The spa weekend, Rialto Ranch for two, please. She bites.

I pick her up half 'n hour late in the new black Land Raker with tiger bars, CD, AC, sunroof, and, natch, car cell. I figured, no way this babe's doing two hours in my Camry and got Faisal to trade me for the weekend. The move pays big. Chelsea doesn't show it exactly, but I can tell she's blown away. Slide in the latest track from Salacios J.O.B., and we are rollin'. Admittedly, not a lot to say at first. It occurs to me at about the ten that I wouldn't even know her last name if I hadn't looked it up in the pig book and since then I've forgot. So I ask her, and she disses, "Starlot, freak." I guess she expected me to remember it. Note to self: don't ask that again. These hotties can be little bitches if you're not on your toes.

We arrive just in time for sunset. Private villa, dropped a suitcase of cake from the Kilimanjaro account, but chicks like Chelsea expect the cream or you're dead meat. I consider it an investment; the players on hand here see me with prime résumé material like Chelsea and they know I'm the deal. Rialto was unbelievably styling. View of the whole fucking desert for miles. Once she sees the room and she's on me before the other shoe could drop. Room service with a smile. Life doesn't get much better'n that. Girl is A-list and a bag of chips. After a few tours of her exotic locales, I do the honorable thing, and pull out a script.

I had read through Stu's heist piece once to get a feel for the thing, but now was time to uncap the red felt tip. With a little guidance from Kilimanjaro Prods., Little Stuey might just have a chance here. But while watching Chelsea change into her swim bikini, it occurred to me if dweezer Bluminvitz took out one of his loser hoods and replaced him with a woman, the whole concept would click. It was simple, but sometimes the obvious ideas are my best. Totally reinventing Tarantino and Esterhaus by going woman—now suddenly there's sexual tension, the whole gender discussion to play with and a chance to show off a bit of tail. I really want to see Stu explore that. Can he write the female voice? I'll get someone else to if he can't. Partial credit? Story by . . . Stu Bluminvitz and Eric Whitfield. Eric Whitfield and Stu Bluminvitz. This script has potential for hugeness.

CHELSEA

Dude, I have scored so major you won't fucking believe it. I've got Eric Whitfield doing so many somersaults for me that I'm going to have to cut him in for 10 percent of my next check. (*Not!*)

The morning after we met at Bud's, he starts speed dialing me at 8:00 A.M. I don't think this guy sleeps. I give him a hard time. I mean get real, it's not his twenty-five-year-old receding hairline that I'm fucking him for. But the loser's got such a hard-on to prove himself to me that he offers to take me to Rialto Ranch Spa for the weekend, which is like the top fucking spa in the whole state. My friend Josie, who's escort agency services only million-per-year-plus execs, gets taken there all the time and said it rips. So despite my better judgement about going back to the well with a wannabe who still hasn't shown me what hand he's holding, I agree to go.

We drive out in Whitfield's so-so Land Raker and the whole way he's playing me these mix tapes of some incredibly lame white rappers who he says he's going to produce after he makes his next film. (Why does every East Coast Jewish boy with a BMW in this town think he's a gangsta?) I just stare out the window, thinking about what an awesome massage and facial I'm going to get and try to ignore Whitfield gettin' funky, rapping along with the tapes. About an hour into the desert, he tries to get me to join in.

"Fft. Awwww night, ba-beee."

To block him out, I try this trick Morton taught us. I light a match and stare into the flame, pretending it's my power. I'm almost calm when the match burns down to my finger, scarring me. The trick works better with a lighter. Or a candle.

"Fft. Gonna take you on awww nigh ba-bee."

"Whitfield. Shut up." I'm trying to remain calm.

"Come on. Do it awww night. You know the thing, sugah."

"Shut up."

"*Do it* with me *awwwww night*," he screams.

"Goddamn it!" I lose it. I'll take a lot from a wannabe producer, but four hours of full-blast rapping in the middle of the desert is lower than my standards sink.

I pulled the face off his stereo and threw it out the window. It took him a few seconds to quiet down enough to realize he was rapping a cappella. "Whoa, bitch. You burned ma box! Wassup pulling that freaky shit on me?"

"Okay" I explained. "New rule. It's bad enough looking at you without having to listen. So from now on, we keep our mouths shut. Or should I hitch home from here?"

He shut up and stayed shut up.

At least he's not Persian, but I was getting truly sorry that I didn't pack any treats for the trip. Probably for the best. Anything lighter than black tar wouldn't have helped with the Whitfield problem.

He booked us a pretty decent suite at the spa with a full-on bar, cable, and in-room Jacuzzi, but two seconds in the door, he practically lacerated my tank top trying to rip it off me. So I fucked him and got it over with (I can stand two-and-a-half minutes of anything). Then I went downstairs to check out who's at the outdoor Jacuzzi.

The scene at the spa was pretty dead. I think everyone's in Toronto for the festival this week. I'll bet Whitfield got the suite at a discount. I just mellowed out and got a massage. Afterwards I baked in the Jacuzzi for two full hours, staring into the desert and thinking about how far I am from my "friends" back in Indiana.

Somewhere out across that sand and a thousand miles at Cormfedd, those fuckers are beating up their wives and kids, and wondering whatever happened to little Chelsea Starlot. Well, don't touch that dial, I almost say out loud. You'll find out soon enough.

While I'm soaking, I see Daisy, this other girl I used to room-mate with. We pretend not to know each other. She still owes me four hundred dollars for the phone bill. I need the cash bad but it's worth letting it slide to have that psycho coke slut out of my life. She's with some Saudi guy who claims to be a prince. Thank God I don't have to do that. Not this month anyway.

Whitfield goes ape shit over this lame-dog script he's got but when I start going cold on him again, refusing to give him his one hundred and twenty seconds worth, his brain reattaches itself to his skull and he says, "You know what this script could use? A really great female action heroine." Like, no duh.

I check my voice mail and Jerry's nephew left a message, say-ing he wants to get together Sunday night, so I tell Whit that we've got to book back to the city early. He sulks and starts beg-ging me to stay, but when I tell him I'll just grab a ride with Daisy and the prince, he gets moving.

From *KENNEL BREAK*
Notes by ERIC WHITFIELD

FREDO
Ah, small problemo, Stiggs. Case you haven't been paying attention here, the door is locked.

STIGGS
Is it?

Stiggs pulls a sardine can out of his sharkskin suit and starts jimmying the back window with the opener.

(NOTE: Sharkskin suit? I wonder. How about smoking jacket?)

FREDO
(impressed)
Sardines. Very nice.

STIGGS
I love sardines, Fredo. They build up a man's gray cell count. All fish do, but none more so than the sardine.

A ghostly howl comes from within.

(NOTE: Wouldn't complete silence be even eerier. I mean, we expect barking, right? Where you're thinking "A," try to go "B" sometimes. That's a little trick I learned. It's yours for free.)

FREDO
What the hell was that?

Stiggs gets the window open and they peer inside. The dogs are all staring back at them curiously.

FREDO
Uh, sit. Good boy.

STIGGS
Which one's Scoob?

FREDO
I don't know, James Bond. I thought you knew
what he looked like.

STIGGS
I do. But the dog was a puppy then. Call its
name or something.

(NOTE: Stu, what is goin' on here with this dog stuff, where's the
funny hit man talk? Let's focus on funny hit man, okay? That goes
for the rest of this scene! Come on, Stu—*borrring!* Get on with it.)

The two hoods climb the sill and drop down into the
pound.

FREDO
Did you know the Japanese take a hot bath every
night before going to bed? But the whole family's got to do it. So they go in one at a time, and
each guy's gotta go in the water the last guy used.

STIGGS
Wait a minute. Why don't they just refill it?

FREDO
You'd run out of hot water.

STIGGS
Hold it. Let me get this straight. They get in a
dirty tub?

FREDO
That's exactly right.

(NOTE: Yes, Stu, yes! This is why we pay you the big bucks! The bath stuff is genius! Is that true? Don't tell me, I love it either way. Here's to the high life, my man!)

DATELINE 2000: BLUMINVITZ. STU.

I got my script back from Whitfield with his notes. He likes it a lot. I guess. He has a few thoughts, though. To tell the truth, he's suggesting some pretty major changes. In fact, they completely destroy my crucial two guys from the neighborhood who grew up together but can't stand each other back story that was the whole point of the script in the first place. He says I've got to let that go. He says I've got to make Stiggs a woman from the same neighborhood, who was kind of a tomboy and is now growing up. A woman? And he wants me to change the sharkskin suits, can you believe it? I think I should draw the line here. I mean, if I cave on this, the whole heist story will be the next thing to go. McKee says stick by your guns. Should I try to call him? Get an insider's perspective?

Okay. Down to Earth again. The Pit Bull just called and told me to stop whining and get writing, but of course he won't have a couch if I don't take this deal. I scoped out a new pad (one bedroom, kitchenette), on Stanley by the farmer's market where Pit Bull and I always go for fry cups. Pit Bull's gonna move in with me until he gets back on his feet. The rent's six hundred and fifty dollars a month but Whitfield's seed money should cover that until the film is released and I come in for the real cash.

Oh God, what should I do? If Stiggs is a woman I just feel like a lot of the bonding scenes are gonna have to be cut. That's what this is about, boy meets boy all over again. Doesn't he get that? Hang on. Got a call.

You're not going to believe this. That was Chelsea on the

phone. Amazing luck! Don't ask me how, but she read *Kennel Break* over the weekend. I must have dropped a copy at her door the day I stopped by impulsively. You know me, right? Anyway, she loved it. This script is making friends! She says that it's so weird Whitfield had the same reaction. She also thinks the Stiggs role should go female too. And, if I'm not mistaken she'd like a shot at the role. Hey, did you hear the one about the Polish actress . . . ? I'm just kidding, I totally respect her. But seriously, it looks like I'll have to make the change.

At the end of the day, Whitfield loved my Japanese bath dialogue. That is my calling card. No one can touch my wiseguy banter. Who cares if it's delivered by a woman—Fredo was really my voice all along.

Got to go. I'm getting together with the Pit Bull for a cap at the Onyx so we can check out their new Japanese comic book art installation.

Four

GRAF SPEE PROD.
Eric Whitfield
President of Production

I've spent the whole day trading calls with Todd Hirtley. This is it, I am landing the big burrito, the tip-top young lit man of the number-one agency on planet Earth. Since his Wolf Pack took control of Neutron, Hirtley's become the only man in lit. He's got a poppin' rep as a closer with a silk pipeline straight to Jerry you-know-who. I got an in with him via Bud who plays Tuesday-night hoops with Hirtley's assistant, Ted Wadsworth, who I set up with some lines in the john at the Whiskey Bar. It's key to know the guy on the desk. I knew I could count on Wadsworth for the proper reminder when I called this morning. Those lines were powdered gold.

I was here when Hirtley called back, but I let the machine pick up. You never answer after you've called and been told he'll call back. You always call back the callback or you're toast. So, I called back later and Hirtley, no slouch, has got to call me back. In the meantime, going over our rewrite:

KENNEL BREAK
by
Stu Bluminvitz and Eric Whitfield

EXT. THE POUND—NIGHT

An ominous howl pierces the night. TWO small-time hoods, FREDO, a junk-food pallored Jersey boy shoots STIGGS—a tough-as-nails blond knockout with a wit to match—a nervous glance.

> STIGGS
> We're goin' in.

> FREDO
> Ah, sure. No offense to your gender and all, but that door's locked.

> STIGGS
> Is it?

Stiggs pulls a sardine can out of her Wonder Bra and starts jimmying the back window with the opener.

> FREDO
> (impressed)
> Sardines. Very nice.

> STIGGS
> I love sardines, Fredo. They build up a woman's physical stamina. All fish do, but none more so than the sardine.

> FREDO
> I've read that.

Stiggs has almost got the window open when Fredo's reflection in the glass arrests her attention.

> STIGGS
> Fredo . . . haven't we met before? I mean before tonight?

Fredo's face becomes a mask a confusion and anxiety.

> FREDO
> I don't know. Do you like karaoke?

> STIGGS
> Not in this lifetime. Were you at Riker's with my Uncle Skeet?

> FREDO
> Nope.

> STIGGS
> I know it's there, something between us . . . but what?

> FREDO
> When I was a little boy in Queens—

> STIGGS
> Queens!

Whoa, there's the phone. It's got to be Hirtley.

"Hey, will you hold for Todd Hirtley in the car?" It's his assistant, Ted Wadsworth.

"Hey, whassup, Wadsworth? How you livin', G?" Always do the man on the desk a solid.

"Uh, fine. Will you hold for Todd?"

"Sure, I can do that. . . ." You bet your ass I will.

After about two minutes he comes on. He must be on the ten or something; the connection's a wind tunnel, but I got him. Same-day return too; the old juice is still flowing.

"Yeah?" he asks.

"Hey, Todd. Eric Whitfield. Friend of Bud's, we met through Chip Kirkoff one night?"

"Chip?" He sounds nervous. "What's this about?"

"As you've no doubt heard, I've got a few projects set up around town. *Cross Four* is this close to a green light, Costner attached to direct supposedly, fine with me, but what I wanted to lay on you is . . . are we on a secure line?"

"I'm on a car cell phone; what do you think?"

"I'm only talking about the next hottest spec sale of the year."

"And?" He's hooked. I got him.

"Not on the phone, Todd. I'm telling you this thing is cashish."

"Call my office. Set up a meeting. Ted, are you there, dipshit?"

"Yes, sir."

"Set up a meeting with . . ."

"Eric Whitfield," I say. Jesus, this guy doesn't let you off easy.

"Yeah, set a meeting with Rick Whitfield. Not a lunch. Not this week. Not more than a fifteen-minute slot. Have you got Jerry's nephew holding yet? Let's go. We're rolling calls, we're jamming, fuck nuts!"

Click.

That could have gone better I guess, but a little humiliation's the price of using the best. They're busy. Shit, the guy had Jerry's nephew on the line.

All right, homies, it's game time now. Need to come in strong to Neutron. Make a name. Whoa, I got it! Yes! The Stiggs role's perfect for Chelsea, right; so I bring her in to the Hirtley meeting like it's all part of Graf Spee Prod.'s package. That fires Chelsea up, keeps her on my speed dial, and Hirtley sees I'm

A-list. No more phone tag, no more chump treatment. If you roll with the wool, you crank with the bank. I call Chelsea. Get the machine. Better call Stu. Tell him our little script's flying high!

CHELSEA

To do: Get new manager
        bumpy skin
        cigarettes?

Fuck. Okay, I've been going all night and it's been the hugest day ever so let me just get it all down. When I am going to change my number, I don't know, but if that serial killer Stu calls once more, I'm going to the MCI police like this. Anyway, it was about 3:30 when Whitfield called to tell me about his big-deal meeting. I was like, "Yeah? What meeting, asshole?" But it turned out it was with Hirtley at Neutron who is supposedly en route to being huge in lit, but also reps some talent, so I said yeah, maybe I'll come.

I get changed into my nylon, V-necked, baby blue, *Got Milk?* baby T and put on the most uncomfortable pair of spiked heels I can find. Whitfield picks me up in a cheap black two-door Camry. What a geek. And he's got Deepak Chopra tapes in the car; am I supposed to be impressed by the depths of his spirtualosity? Whatever. I can get a head trip from the Scientologists any time I want, thank you very much.

Anyway, Neutron is way cooler than I thought it would be. It's in this kicking designer building with a godlike atrium for a lobby, not some fucking third-floor doctor's office shit hole like my first manager Weisenacre and Whatever; this place was wholly tripping. The parking attendants looked like newscasters on that Mexican TV show. They were cut and had these suave mustaches and Ray Bans, not that I would ever—p'lease! Believe it or die. I've still got some standards. Outside Hirtley's third-floor office, it's welcome to unbelievable view, gray carpet, rounded surfaces magazine-fantasy fuck pad. I knew I was going to blow Todd Hirtley even before I've met him.

Twenty minutes later, it's so much for Whitfield. We're in a halogen 100 percent high-end room with Mondrians everywhere, and acres of leather. As suits go, Hirtley's even cuter than Mercy said and he's got this sexy lisp. He takes off his jacket and leans back so I can make out the contours of his pecs through his shirt. Whitfield's blabbing about the script like anyone cares what he thinks. He's kissing so much ass it's embarrassing, but Hirtley's not even listening, he is looking right at my baby T.

Whitfield's like oblivious though. "It's a heist, but completely unique. Are you ready? Buddy number two's a woman? Hello, a woman. Home run, right?"

Hirtley goes, "A woman. Yes, I like it. A woman, good stuff, right."

I mean, yeah . . . who thought of that? Me, not that hackhole Whitfield so I go, "Actually Todd, that was my idea."

And he's all, like, panting now, "Really." Oh, yeah, it was.

Whitfield tries to get back involved with something lame like, "And I think the role would be perfect for a young undiscovered like Chelsea. . . ." Undiscovered when, you chump? Like five minutes ago when I still knew you!

But I only say, "I've done a lot of work, actually. You just haven't seen it."

"I think I have. I see everything and it's my business to remember faces," Todd says.

"You probably noticed my walk-on in *Jerry Maguire*. It was nonspeaking but you'd be surprised how many people have noticed it."

"Probably. I've got a good eye for walk-ons." I've got to tell Morton about that. He got me that role with one phone call.

Hirtley sends Whitfield out with his assistant, "Shit cranny," to get his stub validated and tells me to meet him at his Hummer in the exec parking lot, five minutes. Done. I tell Whitfield I've got to get waxed at Klinger's next door, which makes him really hot, and tell him to pick me up there later. And if I'm not there, I order him, keep waiting, I don't care how long. Loser. Omigod, Hirtley's Hummer Vee was red and only about forty feet long! Hello, I am going to be *huuge!*

THE NEUTRON AGENCY
Memo: # 14471

Note to self. Minus assistant. I need to input this record on my own. Get honest with myself. Clear the brain of some troubling thoughts.

I've been thinking about me all morning. It's good to be Todd Hirtley. Around town, I am known as an animal. In my office, I'm called "Kahn," as in the Persian conqueror, or just "Sire." I have the single hardest abs in the talent agency business. I have the tightest ass. I have buns of steel. Above all others, I have the will to win, at any cost.

Lunched at the Mandarin today with the Wolf Pack. Front-window table, put it on the tab. We've got a minor PR breech. Fourth partner, Karl Salami, gone degenerate apeshit on some grapefruit 45 pills and no longer viable. He's been AWOL for three days. We've been funneling his clients to Rosen, who's in a down cycle at the moment. But word of his unraveling has trickled back. He was spotted walking the Sunset Strip at 3:00 A.M. in his bathrobe, crying to himself like a baby.

Esquire's doing a piece on the supposed coke-fueled break-down. I was the one who leaked the coke stories. At least there's some *cajones* in blow—this puke has got himself loused up on some diet pills. Awful for the image. We are a Wolf Pack, not some sissies OD'ing on Dexatrim, for Christ's sake.

Esquire snoop on the line wants to know why we rehired Salami when we knew all about the problem. I'll read him the entire *Art of War* bit on the flying flank but this story is getting out of control. We've got to get the net on Salami and send the little cocksucker off to Iron John weekends and Outward Bound until Christmas. And no, we won't let him quit, no way. He quits and the whole world finds out what a little sniveling woman he is. Not viable. The boys of Neutron are party pigs with balls of steel! Back when the Wolf Pack first joined forces, the press fingered Salami as our leader. Now, the picture is beginning to clear up as to whom the Il Duce of this team really is.

There were fortune cookies at lunch. Got that same one. Recurring cookie message about, "Friends long absent are coming back to you." Christ, who is it? That summer intern from Cape Cod I fired? Long absent, long absent . . . ? The Pack and I headed back to camp walking three abreast, Boss suits, ties lifting in the air—we are animals, damn it, we party till 3:00 and arrive at the office by 7:00! And we *always* keep it together.

Meanwhile, managing Salami damage control is costing me big-time with the Drain launch. Despite all the prep work, the reaction has been tepid, at best. Yes, we are getting some bids, but not everyone is bidding. Worst of all, Deana botched her end at Hotatsi and the rumor is out that Jerry has banned all future Neutron projects from the lot thanks to her. Talk like that does not add to the Hirtley luster, but I've got my hands so full at the moment, there is not much I can do about it.

Had to squeeze in an after-lunch, predrinks with this slick-dick producer, Whitfield. The guy says he's got a game show setup at Zeus World—my dong-head assistant set up the meeting and forgot to remind me to cancel. Remember to kick his ass good. Whitfield brings some young cokehead chick in a spandex mini who parties at Bud's with him and I make them wait while Ezekiel finishes my shoes. Best damn shoeshine in town. If Salami got more shines we'd never be in this shit. With a good shine, this town's a straight lay.

I send for Whitfield and the chick. Is this a joke? The baggy black two-button suit, white open collar, shades—Long Island white-Jew-rapper-speak, "Hirtley, my man, whassupp?" I'm gonna cancel on him right there but the chick—I mean here's a piece of ass. I love—love—her hair. It's so greasy and wild and untamed. And yet so perfect.

I take the meeting. "Let's do business." Can't focus, the script's an eighth-generation Tarantino rip-off Whitfield's co-written with someone named Bluminvitz who sounds suspiciously like the kid I had ejected from this very office not a month ago, but all I can think about is the sparkle lipstick this skirt has on and how perfectly it matches her purple glitter nail polish.

After eleven minutes of this crap I'm so goddamn ready for that baby blue T that I end the meeting and pull Chelsea into my office again. We arrange to meet down at my Hummer in five. I roll calls on the way back to the place. Rick Drain's belly-aching about his blowhard script. And who's fault is it that Drain dropped the ball? He didn't bring us his best work. Now, he's got to pay the price.

"What're we gonna do, Todd? I'm counting on Neutron, but if they can't make the deal . . ."

"Right. Gotcha. Gonna close the deal first thing tomorrow, baby." Check. Click. Deal with Drain later, I'm on Spalding, pulling into my driveway, and—hold my calls—we're here.

I need to get her out of those clothes, now. I flick on the hot tub, then get the Laker game on the 56-inch, open some Amstels. I've got Deana Cohen's bikini in my dresser drawer that I bring out for Chelsea to change into but she's already naked and in the tub when I get back.

She looks up at me, water glistening on her shoulders. "Nice tub," she says. "Too bad you can't crank up the jets any higher."

"I'll be upgrading to the '98 model in the fall," I assure her. "Adjustable jets come standard."

She nods and keeps staring at me. I'm trying to maintain eye contact while searching with my peripheral for her shirt. I love that shirt. I need to be in that shirt.

She asks, "So, you gonna stand there gasping like an ape all night or are you coming in?"

Fuck, I can't deal with her now. I need to get into a pulsate shower and pull on that baby T. Then I can relax, unwind, maybe get ready to entertain this bitch.

"I have to check the VCR," I say. "One of my clients, has a guest spot on *Arli$$* that I need to tape."

"Who?" she asks.

"No one who matters," I say and rush into the living room, where I find the T lying on the couch. I grab it and rush into the guest bath.

Doorbell! I'm in the shower. Oh, God. The shirt. It's soaked. What am I gonna tell her? Gotta get rid of the shirt. Stuff it in the drawer with Deana's crap. Give her one of mine. Where is she? What the fuck?! And who is at my front door at this hour? Chelsea's getting it.

Oh, holy fuck! It's Jerry's nephew. I invited him over at that Morris party for Luc Besson, but why didn't he phone? Remain calm. War face. Fortress of Steel. I put on my navy bathrobe and light a cigarette before entering, "Hey stranger."

Jerry's nephew looks up from Chelsea, whom he seems to know, takes the cigarette from my lips, and sucks on it. Chelsea, for some reason, starts gathering up her clothes to go. "Where's my shirt, Tad?"

"What?"

"You took it into your bathroom, remember?"

I laugh like she's got to be joking. "Uh, no I did not . . ."

Suddenly, I realize she's found my grandmother's diamond earrings and is wearing them. Jerry's nephew is staring at me and I don't know for sure what the hell he wants at this hour but I do know that I really don't need any stories getting out right after Karl Salami and the diet-pill disaster. Now the little crack whore is fondling my diamond earrings in front of me. She knows. "So, cranberry juice, anyone?"

After two cran and Perriers each, and half my good cheese from Chalet Gourmet, they finally leave, Chelsea taking a ride down the hill with Jerry's nephew. It must have been 2:00 A.M. before I sat down with the Whitfield script. Chelsea's shirt had dried out a little and I snuggled up with what proved to be an utter and complete piece of shit. However, just as I was on the verge of feeding it to my neighbors' brown lab, the phone rang.

"Are you wearing it, Todd?" It was her.

"What are you talking about? And who told you it was all right to call very important agents at this hour. I could have you—"

"Save it for the judge." She cut me off. "I know what you did with my shirt. You're not fooling me with your party pig game, Mr. Very-Important-Agent."

"Listen, you little tramp. If you want to pursue your delusions—"

"No, you listen. I know who you are now, Hirtley. And if you want to keep our little secret quiet, I want some major career cooperation, pronto. My friend Daisy has a date with Baumgarten from ICBM tomorrow night and I've got a little story that they'd just love to chew up."

Baumgarten. That bastard has been after me for years. Paranoid delusions or not, she had me cornered. "What do you want?" I said, sighing.

"I want a part, speaking. A lead would be nice. How about cracking open that script with the part written expressly for *moi* and seeing what you can do with it."

"I will look into it," I said and hung up. *Kennel Break* might have been a loser, but I knew that night that I, Todd Hirtley, was going to have to make it a reality, or else. Loose lips sink ships, and Chelsea's collagen-enhanced kisser looked to be the loosest that I had allowed across the threshold of Castle Von Hirtley. A breach in security, to be sure. But this might still play out to my advantage.

DEANA

You guys, I am dead serious this time. I am so far beyond stressed that if I do not set aside some time to pay attention to myself, I *will* freak. Do you know what I mean? My friends at home say that Hollywood is all about movie stars and glamour and sushi, but I'm all like, no you guys, it's not. It's hard work.

I hear Club Med has this deal where you pay a discount rate (which I totally need because my credit card debt is approaching, like, the stratosphere) and you get on a plane and they surprise you with which Club they take you to. That is exactly what I need. Two weeks on some nameless beach, having sex with the snorkeling instructor or a vacationing dentist. How perfect would that be right now? I am all about taking care of myself.

Why is it so impossible to get anything serious done in this town? To get the ball rolling today, I am being deluged by these losers who are blaming me for having their pay cut. I cannot get a single script read because they are ringing my phone off the hook, yelling at me like it's my fault for bringing Jerry a script by the most up-and-coming writer in town. So, I'm just like, look, maybe if you guys would take Jerry's advice and do some work instead of spending all day composing me nasty E-mails then you *might* just get ahead here someday. After all, that's what I am trying to do! Anyway, I know the real reason they're calling is to get my attention. I swear, I feel like I've rejected half the guys on the lot this month alone.

But seriously, I thought Jerry was going to lose it after he read the Drain script and visions of grad school were dancing in my head. He's totally right though, animals are the perfect high-concept vehicles for vertically integrated companies. Animals and women. I think women are the new market that is going to take over. *Girlfriends* opened at 24 million dollars without even an A-list name. If it kills me, I am going to get this studio to make a serious film that gives women their place in the movies, addresses real contemporary social issues, and does phenomenal at the box office.

Speaking of women's issues, on top of my daily stack I had to do a Brown alumni interview this morning. I was meeting my candidate at the Sunset Plaza Coffee Bean. I went early, hoping to get some reading done away from the ringing phone, but that was wishful thinking because who should I see at the next table but this really gross though kind of cute producer guy, Eric Whitfield, who I met at Kayla's birthday dinner at Bud's. When I met him, he was totally wasted and tried to get me to go to Two Bunch for the weekend with him and I was like, thanks but no thanks in this lifetime. He totally played off the whole thing and comes over and is like, "Hey, wassup, Dee! The Cohenator!"

And I'm like, "Whatever, Whitfield. Could we do this later because I really have to work."

But he won't leave. "Dea-na! My wo-man. You got to get a piece of this gangsta spec I got coming. It is the *bomb*."

"Yeah, what I really need in life is another spec to read. Speaking of which, oops, look at the time. Gotta work. Bye." He hovered above my table for a few minutes before finally sliming away. I tried again to read but my interviewee showed up two minutes later.

I gotta say, I felt sorry for the poor girl. She has super grades and extracurriculars, but she didn't have that thing that

Brown students have—you know, the edge. I could tell right away she wasn't getting in when she walked up with this ridiculous mall hair, like a *chola* tank top and these nerdy, thick black glasses and asks me straight off what Brown's premed program is like. Her name is Cindy Closenacher and she goes to the Brentwood School. Normally I would have ended it right away and just told her she should think about, maybe, Northeastern, but her father is Alan Closenacher, the head of movie tie-ins for Del Taco, so I decided to be nice and give her the full interview.

"Why do you really want to go to Brown?" I asked her.

"I got two of my Westside homies there now and they are down with the Providence scene. I'm also wanting to study premed and I hear it's a killer science program."

I take a deep breath. "Okay, first of all. Brown students do not hang out in Providence. Providence is like, verbatim, or verboten or whatever to Brown students."

"No way man, my homegirls say the scene is fresh. They went raving last—"

"Look, I don't know what your homies told you, but I went to Brown and my best friend from freshman year dated a townie, who knocked her up and she had to drop out of school and now is like, an office manager at an insurance company or something."

"Harsh."

"That's right. So, no Brown students hang out in Providence. Second, if you want to be premed, I really think you ought to consider, like, a technical school. Brown is for students who are there to question our basic cultural assumptions, who are willing to dissect stereotypes and examine the dominant paradigms. Is that what you want to do?"

"Ummmm . . . what do you do with a degree in that?"

I was getting truly pissed. "It's not about getting a taxicab license, it's about learning how to challenge the status quo."

"Is that what you do for work now?"

"Yes, I work in development. I look for scripts that, you know, try to do something more . . . like make a statement about the culture and try to subvert . . ."

"Cool, what movies did you make?"

"I was involved in the early stages of *Connect the Dots.*"

"Oh, the one with the gorilla?"

"Did you see it?"

"On cable. What was that subverting?"

"Look, you little snot, the original script had a totally unique take on the concept of a game movie and a flawless structure. But we got stuck with a first-time director and the writer who couldn't take notes!"

"Chill, lady. I'm just asking!"

"Don't call me *lady*. I'm only twenty-six years old!"

"All right, all right. So are you looking for a high school movie?"

"Who isn't? Why?"

"I've been working on a pitch with ma crew."

"Really? Okay, hit me." And it turned out her pitch was pretty good. Falls apart midway through the second act but a great setup and she is really good with character arc. Not Brown material, but I'm having her in for another pitch next week.

On my way out, I noticed Whitfield chatting up Cindy and getting her number. I hope he didn't hear the pitch.

After work, I stopped by Todd's house. Jerry's nephew was leaving as I got there and Todd was really beat and so was I, so we just went to sleep and I didn't even make him do anything.

Todd mentioned that he has another action script he is looking at that might be promising, but after the Rick Drain debacle, I'm not sure I want to see another script from him ever again.

From KENNEL BREAK
Notes by TODD HIRTLEY

EXT. DOG POUND—NIGHT.

Fredo and Stiggs sneak to the back wall and pull tools out
of a burlap satchel.

FREDO
Remember when you set the timer too early
and the Weasel blew his hand off?

STIGGS
(Taking a bite of a submarine sandwich.)
The guy was late. Whatcha gonna do?

(**NOTE:** We should *never* see Stiggs eating.)

FREDO
Whatcha gonna do? Scooby Doo, where are you?

STIGGS
So, when you last make a pipe bomb anyways?

(**NOTE:** Why Stiggs? I like . . . *Natasha*.)

FREDO
What, you worried? I grew up building these
things!

STIGGS
You grew up getting whacked on the head by
your mama.

(NOTE: Why is it a pipe bomb? We can raise the stakes here. What if they are building an atom bomb?)

> FREDO
>
> Watch it sister, or I'll see you get whacked in a minute.

> STIGGS
>
> So you in on that Mighty Mart job last week?

> FREDO
>
> Not sayin' I was.

> STIGGS
>
> Heard they made off with two hundred cartons of Winstons.

> FREDO
> (lighting up a cigarette)
> Smoke 'em if you got 'em.

They both laugh, hard.

(NOTE: Why do we care about a convenience-store theft? The budget on this film is too limited to justify a huge script purchase price. This small-time angle is way off. Make them international jewel thieves, glamorous, young, sexy. Think *Hart to Hart* but younger and criminals.)

DATELINE BLUMINVITZ EXPRESS 2000

I am learning about this business the hard way, but that's how all the greats got started. You pay your dues, study at the school of hard knocks, and then get to make projects that are really important to you. Just look at Kevin Smith.

Things are going great for *Kennel Break*. Mr. Whitfield gave it to Todd Hirtley, who is the premier literary agent for edgy young writers. I've been trying to get him to look at my stuff for years, but couldn't get in the door. Last time I tried, they called security. But apparently he and Whitfield are really tight and Whitfield gave him a copy of *KB*. I know he'll love it. Hirtley is the man to take this Bluminvitz to the top.

What's more, I am finally out on my own. With all the dough I am expecting from the script, I spread my wings and got my own place. It's a really cool studio on Sierra Bonita between Fairfax-La Brea-Melrose-Beverly. This is *the* neighborhood to live in. The Pit Bull calls it "Gen X Auschwitz" but to me it's a hot, bustling intellectual melting pot like Greenwich Village in the fifties or the Haight in the sixties. About eight guys from my class at Reed live on the same block and we still hang out a lot. Hollywood insiders call us the Reed Mafia since the school has spawned such an amazing number of hot and edgy young writers. And it looks as though I'm going to be the first of the bunch to break through. I swear, though, I'll bring the others with me once I'm on the inside.

Speaking of the Pit Bull, he was evicted from his place so I'm letting him crash with me for a while. It's pretty cool having such a great figure from old Hollywood living on my couch. My one room is pretty crowded between my seventies lunch-box collection and his boxes of classic girlie magazines (he dated most of the centerfolds back in the fifties and gets sentimental about his old flames) but we are getting by. We had one small incident, though. The landlord stopped by to pick up my deposit and the Pit Bull told him to get lost or he'd tear his head off and then pushed him down the stairwell. I straightened things out and told him the Pit Bull was just visiting. I have to type quietly now because he is passed out on the floor next to me. You know these hard-drinking Hemingway types.

On the downside, while I'm waiting for the *Kennel Break* money to pour in, I've had to take a temp job to cover the rent. I've been answering phones at the Hotatsi Studio. It's a pretty cool job, working right at the center of the action, but there is this one girl who works there named Deana who I don't think is a huge Bluminvitz fan. She got a call from some guy who wouldn't give his name, just said he was someone's nephew, so I took a message instead of transferring him.

When Deana saw the message, she went postal on me and started yelling, "Oh, my God! Which idiot hired another writer to answer phones? This is so completely lame, we might as well just shut down!" Kind of harsh, but she said she was having a day from hell.

Hang on, there's someone at the door—

That was strange. Whitfield just dropped the script with Hirtley's note on it through my mail slot and then drove off before I could talk to him. I chased his car for a few blocks. I guess he didn't see me. He left a note on top of the script saying, *Stu, my man. Got to make these changes by 9:00* A.M. *manana. I know you can do it. You're mah boy.—EW*

I am kind of surprised by Hirtley's notes. For a guy who handles Rick Drain, he sure seems to want to take the edge off the script. He wants to make the hoods international jewel thieves now. Sort of changes my premise a bit, but I guess this is how we get movies made in the big time. Once I am in the door and start pitching them my ideas, Mr. Whitfield says I'll be able to write my own ticket. The Pit Bull woke up and I showed him Todd's comments and he agreed with them. "Fuck small-time. We gotta think big. There's no room for pygmies at the top!" And then he passed out again.

I think I am going to take my laptop to the Stir Crazy Coffeehouse to rewrite this so I don't wake the Pit Bull up. I better change my outgoing message to tell Chelsea where I am in case she calls and wants to get together. I haven't heard from her lately and her number has changed. I think she must have lost my number. I was at a liquor store on Sunset and saw her head shot hanging above the counter. I left my number and asked the manager to tell her to call me if she stopped in. The Pit Bull said he saw her picture at a dry cleaner on Santa Monica, so I better leave a message there also. It may seem like a lot of hassle, but when something is meant to be, you have to be willing to go to any lengths.

Wow, it's 2:30 already. I better get started. So long, I am off to the big time.

Five

THE NEUTRON AGENCY
Memo: # 14472

Todd Hirtley does not fuck up. Todd Hirtley does not lose. Are you with me, scumatron?

There are two types of players in this business: Those with the juice and the bottom feeders who would sell their parents, grandparents, and third cousins twice-removed for a chance to lick the coffee stains off this agency's hardwood floors.

The word is out that Todd Hirtley has lost his juice. The Rick Drain fiasco must not be repeated. We took our eyes off the ball and we are paying the price. Yes, I know it sold, but to sell is not enough. Squeaking a script through is not acceptable. Every Neutron-handled spec must carry the Todd Hirtley aura of invincibility. Every script that leaves this office with a glossy red Neutron cover must glow with the certainty of concept so high it will blow the roof off your studio commissary and with pieces of casting so enormous that Arnold, Bruce, Mel, and Jean-Claude will be begging for invites to your daughter's bat mitzvah.

Yes, shit for brains, I know we sold it; but word leaked about Jerry's distaste for the project. I was at the Grand Havana Cigar Club last night. I want a humidor there. Get me the one next to

Jonathan Dolgen's. Eric Aibrex has it now but he's not half the agent I am. I want him out and me in. Make it happen. So in the pathetic absence of my own personal humidor, I smoked Whitfield's Cohibas. The loser gets some good cigars somehow. *No!* Do not send him a thank-you note. Call and tell him I want another box by five. Make him understand that kissing the ring of Todd Hirtley is a matter of course, de riguer for the nothings of this world like him. Anyhow, I was playing backgammon with Schwartz from Praxaline and he says, "I hear Drain's script finally sold."

"What do you mean, *finally?* It was a slam dunk!" I say.

"Not with Jerry, from what I hear."

"Jerry loved the script. He was just looking in a different direction for the next major project."

"It couldn't be that heat is off Todd Hirtley on the Hotatsi lot?" he asks.

"The heat is never off Todd Hirtley. Anywhere," I tell him. And to prove my point, I offer him doubles and promptly beat his ass all over the backgammon board—in full view, I might add of Mr. Arnold Schwarzenegger who was playing at the next table. (Send him a thank-you note and flowers today.)

So word is out that your master has lost his juice. Drain called this morning. He heard the rumor that Jerry passed and is so depressed he's not even throwing a spec-sale party.

But we are about to make a comeback with a splash that will soak this town through its underpants. I have reread Whitfield's script and I think it might just be our rocket ship to as yet unreached heights of seven-figure sales. With the new draft, the project is perfect for a Will Smith or Steven Seagal type in the lead with a hot newcomer like Chelsea as the street-smart and sexy action heroine.

I started the wheels turning this morning with a stop by the 7:00 A.M. AA meeting at the Log Cabin. When I walked in, Jim Berkowitz from Verbatim was at the door greeting. I remember reading in the trades that he just got out of Hazelden. Looked like he had about thirty days sober, pretty edgy, raw and vulnerable. Fucker passed on the World War III script I sent out last summer. He stuck his hand out to greet me.

"Hi, I'm Jim. Welcome." Then he recognized me. "Ohhh, Todd. I didn't know you were one of us."

I grabbed him by the collar. "Listen, stink breath. I will never be one of you. And today, I've got problems you couldn't possibly relate to, so just do your damn commitment and stay away from me." Keep the little fuck on his toes. Humiliation will make him want a piece of the script even more.

I arrived early to lock up a good seat, dropping my keys on one directly in front of the leader. Before the meeting started, I milled around in the kitchen by the coffee, looking like a man with the weight of the world on his shoulders. Whenever anyone tried to say hello, I just waved them away, looking like I was fighting back tears.

When the meeting started, I raised my hand to share straight out of the gate. They called on me and I summoned up all the dramatic focus that two summers of acting camp in the Berkshires had taught me. By the time I reached the podium, tears were streaming down my face.

"My name is Todd Hirtley and I'm a grateful recovering alcoholic at the Neutron Agency," I say. "It's a long time since I've shared at the group level, but I had to open up and get honest before my disease takes charge. They say, you're only as sick as your secrets and I've been carrying around the most enormous secret of my life without having the courage to reach out to you people for help with it."

I take a deep breath. The room is with me, on the edge of their seats dying to hear that the great Todd Hirtley could be struck down by the problems of mere mortals.

"I have this script," I said, sobbing, the tears flowing freely. "I think this concept is so original, the leads so castable, the action so intense, so destined for two-hundred-million-plus domestic, that I just know that it will make the career of whoever buys it." Deep breath. Pause.

"But," I said, "I have so many friends who will hate me if I don't give them a chance to buy it. I just don't know where to turn. I hate being in the middle; I hate the power. I need to turn this script over to my higher power, and let Him take charge."

I paused for a full minute, weeping, and then let my face suddenly clear, looked up and smiled. "I know what to do," I told the room. "God just gave me the answer. I need to take care of myself. I'm going to tear up the script, quit the agency, and look for a way I can devote myself to working with others. No more power. No more deciding whose career to make overnight. Thank you all for being here for me. Without this program, I might have just gone out and sent the script to the wrong person and been forced to drink over the agony of not making one of my friends a billionaire. Thank you for letting me share."

I left the podium, grabbed my keys off the chair, and walked straight out the front door. From the parking lot across the street, I could hear the entire meeting reach for their cell phones.

For the rest of the day, I am not in to anyone. Make that for the rest of the week. Tell anyone who calls that I am in Aspen, reviewing my life. At Guber's. With Guber. You got that? Good.

Supposed to meet Jerry's nephew tonight, but I told Chelsea she could stop by also. Call her and find out what she'll be wearing. Suggest the pink-suede pumps. Tell her I like those. Call Deana Cohen and cancel on her. Give her the Aspen story.

I am going on-line. Are you on AOL, piss boy? You should be. Great way to keep your finger on America's pulse without having to leave the 310. Rev me up, I'm going on. No calls for the next forty-three minutes.

DEANA

Todd Hirtley is, I swear, literally the biggest geek I have ever met in my entire life. I mean, I gotta admit he is totally cute but if he thinks another one of his scripts is getting anywhere near Jerry's office via *moi*, then he has been inhaling his hair spray. Besides, I heard that Jerry's nephew is, like, way into some actress and doesn't even talk to Todd anymore. But I'm remembering the D-Girl's motto: Keep your friends close and your loser friends closer because you never know who might have a great concept. Also, Doug, the director of development at Pathfinder, told me his roommate was at a Cocaine Anonymous meeting where everyone was talking about Todd's new script, like it was so hot Todd couldn't take the heat and was smoking crack over it or something.

For all those reasons, I agreed to meet Todd last night at Bud's. He was late, of course, but it was cool because I hung out in the back and watched this monitor Bud installed. It's hooked up to a surveillance camera aimed at the rope line out front and so you can check out all the people getting turned away. I saw this writer dork, who is temping here and totally screwing up our phones, show up with this old homeless guy and argue with the doorman for an hour before he got the hint. And then, just as they are about to give up the homeless guy tries to rush the door and the doorman punches him in his seventy-five-inch waistline, which makes the homeless guy ralph all over him. I swear, it was the funniest thing I have seen in my entire life. God, I've got to make a note to put that scene in the next script I work on.

When I walked in this morning, I ask writer-dork, "Have a good time at Bud's?"

He turned all red and muttered something like, "I was supposed to be on a list."

And I'm all, like, "Which one, the pathetic-loser list?"

Anyway, Todd turned up beyond late, which is completely unacceptable for someone who wants to be a part of my life and who has no clout with Jerry. But he was being all sweet and apologetic, so I didn't bolt out of there. I know, in the future I should. I must demand respect in relationships.

Then he turned on the agenty hard sell and said, "Deana, I'm going to make you the queen of Hollywood."

"Just so long as you don't give me another script or Jerry will make me the welfare queen of Hollywood when he throws me out on my ass."

He sighed, trying to be all dramatic. "Yes, mistakes were made, but I am now in possession of a script so hot that you can go ahead and order your business cards reading 'VP of Production, Deana Cohen.' "

I was choking on my drink with laughter, but I stringed him along just to hear what he had, hoping to fill up another line in the tracking report. "Okay, like, what kind of no-concept gabfest are you pushing today?"

"Deana, you'll have to wait. I'm going away for a few weeks to take stock of my life."

Oh, get real. "Take stock of your life? Where are you going to do that, in the Gucci shoe department?"

He turned redder than my cosmopolitan. "Okay. I'll give you an advance look. But no one hears a word about this. I'm telling you, Jerry is going to do cartwheels over this one. It's called, are you ready, *Kennel Break*."

I really felt sorry for him by now; he's so desperate to get in with Jerry. "All right, give me your stupid script. I'll add it to my stack for this weekend."

"You'll want to read this one tonight."

"I doubt it."

I followed him to his car to get the script. On the way, we, like, almost bashed into Tony Liter, the biggest talent manager and the biggest queer in town, one of the kingpins of the Velvet Mafia. It's so typical of the way women are treated in this town that just when we start getting in the door, the guys at the top all become gay to create a new way to keep the girls out of the club.

But can I just tell you, when Todd saw Tony he started totally fawning over him and doing this ridiculous lisping thing, saying, "Tony, you're suit ith juth gorgeouth. You have to let me buy you a thalad thomeday." Tony gave him a card and brushed him away.

As we walk away, Todd was, like, "Pretty slick, I must say. That *fagela* bought that I was flirting with him hook, line, et cetera." And I'm thinking, even for Hollywood, this must be a new low. Todd, who is so obviously gay, pretending to be straight pretending to be gay. I can't wait to share this with my therapist.

So Todd gave me the script and I'm, like, great, don't call me, yeah, yeah. He saw I wasn't so hot to read it, so he started, like, kissing my neck there in the parking lot and I got kind of turned on and asked him, "Why don't you come over?"

But he pulled back and said, "Don't you want to get through this script tonight?"

And I'm all, like, "whatever" and drive off. Do you know what I mean?

But when I get home and read it, turns out *Kennel Break* is not so bad. I think the female lead could be developed to make this a really interesting female-bonding movie. With a little bit of drama, it could totally tap into the women marketplace. There is no way in hell I am going to show this script to Jerry, but I think I'll work with Todd on it, down the line, who knows. . . ?

From *KENNEL BREAK*
Notes by DEANA COHEN

EXT. COLONIAL MANSION LAWN—NIGHT.

Fredo and Natasha REMOVE their black catsuits, revealing Fredo's TUXEDO and Natasha's EVENING GOWN. They open a black bag and remove a GYROSCOPE.

A party is going on inside the house.

(NOTE: Instead of a black-tie party, shouldn't it be something a little more hip and edgy, like a virtual-sex meeting?)

> FREDO
> With this, I should be able to pinpoint Scooby's precise location within the mansion.

> NATASHA
> Looks like they've got him in the underground arboretum.

> FREDO
> Are you ready? With this crowd, we're bound to run into trouble.

> NATASHA
> I live for trouble.

They EMBRACE and SNEAK across the lawn toward the mansion.

(NOTE: I don't understand why Natasha would run into this

house if she knows that it is so dangerous. Maybe we can put in some backstory here. What if, besides Scooby having the diamonds in his dog collar, Natasha was an orphan and Scooby was her only friend. That might explain why she is bothering.)

As they RUSH across the lawn, Natasha's heels get STUCK on something. As she reaches down to pull her shoe free, Fredo JUMPS at her and KNOCKS her aside.

BOOM!

A land mine EXPLODES beneath Natasha's DISCARDED shoe.

NATASHA
I'll never find another pair to match this dress.

A TEAM of men emerge from the mansion and BEGIN shooting at Fredo and Natasha.

FREDO
If you don't get out of here quick, you'll be looking for pumps in red to match the holes in our heads.

They RUSH off, dodging bullets.

(NOTES: *Yawn!* Can we please raise the stakes here! I mean, we have all seen bullets before. How about lasers or nuclear weapons? Also, this scene would be maybe slightly more interesting if we could find out more about Natasha and what it is like to be an international jewel thief and try to balance a relationship with your career. What if we turn Fredo into a couple of Natasha's girlfriends and give them more opportunity to talk about men.)

DATELINE BLUMINVITZ STREET

Ross, my friend from Reed, says I've gone Hollywood and sold my soul to The Man. I don't think that's true at all. The fact is that when you're dealing with high rollers like Mr. Whitfield and Todd Hirtley, you've got to be willing take some punches, to show them you can play the game; if you want to be taken seriously, that is. Not that I'm exactly showing them anything in person yet. I mean, Mr. Whitfield told me Todd is representing the script, but when I got excited and cried, "I'm in the big time now! Todd Hirtley is my agent!" he tossed a big bucket of cold water on my head.

"Whoah, my man. You gotta chill on this until Whitfield gets it straight for you."

"What do you mean?" I asked. "He's not representing us?"

"Stu, mah boy. A *mucho cajones* player like Hirtley doesn't rep writers, he reps projects."

"But he's repping my project—"

"Our project. I mean, officially my project, based on your idea."

"But when we meet with Todd I'll—"

"My man, I wouldn't start packing your bags for any meetings just yet. Let me see how to play this. You know you're ma homey, I'm looking after you."

"But Todd will—"

"You are forgetting to *fo-cus*. Now I got you some more notes to work in tonight. These come from the studio itself."

"But tonight? My swing-dance lessons are at eight!"

"Stu! Ma boy! If you're going to swim with the sharks, you got to grow some teeth. Forget about swing, my man and I promise to get you straight into SkyBar next week."

"SkyBar? Really? I heard Cameron Diaz hangs out there."

"All the little hotties will be there for my señor *Rico Suave.*

And no rope line either; my man Stu is going straight through the back door."

I know what you're going to say: How could I skip my swing-dance lessons for the SkyBar? How could I even think about walking away from the up-and-coming hot young minds of Los Feliz to hang out with a bunch of phonies on Sunset Strip?

It's a good question, but I have an answer. Once I am in the door of SkyBar, I can pave the way for my friends, the real artists, to follow me. They may say I'm selling out now, but when I am on first names with the doorman at SkyBar, and can bring them along, then we'll see who's sold out. And once we are all in, we can really shake up the system, start making the kind of seriously gritty and edgy films that will scare the hell out of "America" and put the bite back into Hollywood.

Mr. Whitfield gave me notes from a production company and the first thing I noticed is they were written by Deana Cohen, an exec at the office where I temp. The one who keeps yelling at me. And if you thought she was tough in person, you should see her on paper. *Whewwwie.* I must say I seriously considered pulling out of the project for an hour or so. But then the Pit Bull reminded me that if I have to move back in with my parents in Sherman Oaks, I can kiss my chances with Chelsea good-bye.

So I made a few changes. Deana's notes have destroyed the last vestiges of my original Tarantino homage concept. This final draft is more of a *Waiting to Exhale* meets *Con Air* homage. But hey, look at what John Woo is able to do with the action genre and no one accuses him of selling out. Besides, Todd Hirtley, Mr. Whitfield, and Deana Cohen are professionals and I'm lucky to have the opportunity to learn from them.

At work today I decided to let Deana know I had made her changes and have a little tête-à-tête between filmmaking pros. When I walked into her office at lunch, she looked up from her stack of scripts and threw a stapler at my head, screaming, "Get out!"

I told her that I just wanted to say how much I appreciated her notes, She gave me looked very suspicious stare and said, "What notes?"

"On *Kennel Break*?"

"Oh, my God, why were you reading my notes? Did you go through my purse? Oh, my God, I knew you were a freak—"

"No, you don't understand," I explained. "I'm the writer. I'm Stu Bluminvitz."

"Who? What? No, you don't understand. If you don't get out of my office in three seconds I *will* call security and get you banned from the lot forever, you half-wit. *Get out!*"

That probably wasn't the best meeting I'll ever have, but at least I'm in the door. I think I noticed her yelling at me a little less in the afternoon.

I'm really close to finding Chelsea. I followed the Pit Bull's lead to a liquor store at Sunset and Doheny where her head shot hangs right next to Rip Taylor. The manager there told me she comes in to buy a pint of Stoli almost every night. Guess I've got my plans for this evening. God, will she be surprised. Since her number changed, I can only imagine how hard she's been trying to find me.

Uh, oh. The Pit Bull is waking up and will probably want to get to the Formosa before happy hour ends. Gotta run.

CHELSEA

To do list:
Head shots
Skull enlargement
Move
Dr. Yang

Going batshit without my Zoloft. Fucking stringy haired Dr. Elkin won't refill my Rx because she's a dried-up old bag and sits there all hour resenting my body. Lifted five pills off Jerry's nephew, sitting in his Boxster's glove compartment—guy's a total addict. I don't know what they were but they didn't go at all with the tequila shots. Send Hirtley the bill for my bathroom rug. The fruitcake's agenting for me now.

Damn it, I need to score. Have some Xanax '91s. Stale shit, not gonna do it. Gotta find a new Dr. Yang, make an appointment, score. Try the yellow pages. How many fucking head shrinks are there in this town, c'mon!? Pick up, pick up . . .

"Dr. Harmon's office, can I help you?"

"Yeah, does he prescribe Zoloft? To patients and stuff?"

"Well, that would depend. The doctor prefers to work these things out through therapy."

"Jesus Christ, I'll pay, all right. Who is this?"

"This is Neil."

"I want some . . . fuckin' . . . Zoloft . . . Neil!"

"Why don't you come in for an appointment?"

"Do I sound like I have time for an appointment, dickhead?"

Hang up. Goin' out for a while. Drive around. Put up some more head shots. A new dry cleaners just opened on Beverly and I hear their wall is completely bare. Gotta grab it fast. Being the only shot they've got hanging is a definite to get noticed. Gotta relax, get some air. Drive down to Gil Turner's. Give'm the new pix, take down some Anistons, like she needs the space anymore. That cow was in my acting class. Without that prom-queen hair bob she'd still be swabbing tables at De Bevick's. Glance through my new head shots that are kickin' hot, but one of Morton's etiquette police, his Nazi assistants, said I have a small skull. A film star's head-to-body ratio is very high, he says. So Paul Newman, Tom Cruise, Winona—they all have big heads-little bodies, right? It's something about the camera I don't know. Anyway, Lida just got a skull enlargement and it looks freaky in person but her new pics are amazing. People who I would so ignore before with new big heads are now assertive or something. And Lida's fucking career opportunities have only gone through the roof, but she's taking a job in Brunei to live with one of the sultan's brothers or some guy for 175 thou a year and clothes money. She'd rather be a harem slave than fight to get it all. I could have that same job in a second. They've practically begged me. But I'm not giving up yet. I'll do Brunei when I'm thirty, if nothing's happened by then.

I pull up in front of Turner's on the strip. Grab my head shots and jump out.

"Chelsea! Hi!"

I don't believe it—it's my stalker. Steve or Flip or something. And he's with some homeless guy. Probably his dad. He keeps trying to touch my elbow with his knuckles like it's an accident, "Whoa, what are you doing here?"

"I'm working. Look, here . . ." I load him with a stack of my head shots. "I need these put up tonight." Omigod, he's smiling like he's all flattered. *Aagghh*, I have seriously got to move or call the cops. Does Hirtley have a guest house?

I'm going to SkyBar, needed a fucking Stoli yesterday. Victor's not at the door. Line's thirty people deep. I do not need this shit. I push up to the rope.

"Is Victor here?"

"Who?" I hate that bullshit; he knows who I mean.

"Victor. He works here. Every night."

"Not tonight he doesn't."

"I can see that. Listen, I'm meeting friends inside."

He's thinking. It's that key moment. But I'm too tense to flirt right now. He lifts the rope.

"Thanks."

Still got it. Screw the skull enlargement, screw Brunei, screw my manager. Chelsea Starlot needs a drink. The bar is crawling with wankers. Sheik creeps in silk suits. Once they get through the rope line they unbutton their yellow shirts to their hairy navels. It's fucking gross. But they're loaded, I guess. Gold Mercedes, parents are always gone, Nokia cell phone, pockets of coke. Whatever. I recognize half the girls here from Morton Karmellian and various open calls but none of us acknowledge each other. It's like everyone's just goin', "What? I'm not one of them. Those whores." I, for one, am not one of them. I am on the verge of a fucking breakthrough. Believe it.

Some dweeb with an oxford shirt and a Red Stripe gives me the "I'm in CD-ROM, but our first feature's not far off," horseshit. I just walk away. Life's too short. Mine is, anyway. I'm coming through the lobby when I see the Jewish Rock Hudson, Eric Whitfield. What a spank. Anyway, I detour him on an errand to buy me some drugs and blow out of there. Perfect ditch. One more doofus who'll be around if total affliction should befall my life and ever I need to speak to him again. I have class in the morning and my career comes first. *Hasta* assholes!

JAIPUR PRODUCTIONS
Eric Whitfield, CEO

My Eagle has landed. I'm a-rolling with the creme players, marquee names, wired for bid'ness. Ho-yeah. Here's the dope. Back in the day, you'll remember mah boy Stu Bluminvitz, the kid I decided to school? Well, the golden goose has laid another egg right on my doorstep. Jaipur Productions (India is so hot right now) has added a new jewel to the crown. *Kennel Break*, our grunge actioner, has found its target. Todd freakin' Hirtley, the grand master of the Neutron Agency, is salivating all over the brads. It's go-time. Green-light highway. Lalapacruza.

Hold it. Red phone.

Yesss. Holmes is in da house. That was Hirtley. Himself. Not the piss-boy assistant, "Will you hold for Todd Hirtley," but the Man direct and uncut. Here's the game plan. Put your on ears and hear the music. Hirtley's no bullshit.

From the get-go it's like this, "Whitfield, we're going long and deep. I want blockers in the secondary, I want eight men downfield, then on hut, when the numbers run white, I'll call the strike." The man is in one of his classic attack modes, the war face, the locker-room shit, it's legendary. And it's all behind *Kennel Break*.

So, I'm playing it all caj', "I heard that! You got the ball you make the call!"

I may have overdone it because Hirtley tells me "stuff it, and let me handle the business end: You focus on networking. What you're going to do is this: Get on the phone. Now. Call up every Deana, Tonya, and Alyse you know and apologize to them. You want them to know how sorry you are in advance. Because next week Todd Hirtley is going out with your script, and though you begged, though you pled, he said he'd sooner send it to the moon then let them have a look. The moon. Then you hang up. No chatty-Kathy bullshit. This is business, got it?"

Boys, the man is a pro. What's more, the cash supply is again fresh just as the till was almost empty. Once Hirtley hands me the green light, I phone up Jaipur's investors and the boys back home and let them know we've got the muscle behind us.

"I've never heard of this guy," Turf, the stoop tells me.

"That's 'cause you ain't plugged in to know the players," I explain. "That's why you got me in the front office, scoping the scene."

"Okay, so you got this Hirtley guy on board. What do I care? When am I going to see some return?"

"My good man, if this bird flies you can count on return aplenty, multitudinous percentage on your investment."

"Yeah, yeah, yeah. That's what you've been telling us for a year now."

"Homey, I would not lie to you. The route to riches has been a little less direct than I anticipated, but we are almost across the threshold and just need that final push to bring home the gold."

"Final push?"

"We're jumping into sell mode. That means I've got to be able to operate at one-hundred percent capacity."

"That means you need more money."

"My man, I'm giving up more points for it. And that, this late in the game, is grand theft you are taking me for."

"Eric, the boys feel we've given you all we should."

"Of course, I'll require your consultation once we move into production."

"Uh-huh. Right now, we're looking for loss-cutting scenarios, not greater exposure."

"The casting season, of course, will require your participation."

"Casting?"

"All the ingenues, my man. Did you get the photos I FedEx'ed you?"

"Will they be auditioning?"

"And they want to meet the money. Want to real bad."

"Eric, I don't know."

"Then there's the premiere. You fly out and are the toast of the town. That'd be something nice to bring back to the brokerage. When the boys at the office see you escorting A-list betties down the red carpet."

"If this deal doesn't close. . . ."

"And Hirtley's talking Oscar contender."

Sigh. "How much more do you need?"

Deal closed, I head to SkyBar to celebrate. Got a new trick. The place is so crawling with unbelievably fine models that if you're not a fully fledged Tehranian gold smuggler, you can forget the velvet ropes. But if Le Mac, myself, rents a hotel room upstairs for a mere 350 dollars, it's bar passes gratis plus guests, and when you score it's as simple as, "You ever see the rooms here?"

So, I'm checking in, Visa Gold, when who should walk through the lobby on the way to the "powder room" but my fly mama herself Miss Chelsea.

"Hey, girl!"

"What're you doing? Don't you live in L.A.?"

"Hey, yeah. Getting a little roomsky for late night."

"Whatever. Do you have any money?"

"Sure. I got you covered. You're mah girl." These super-hotties can get away with that shit.

"Get out like two hundred. Give it to Connor. Then meet me on the deck." Connor's a stud and a blow dealer.

"All right. Or we could just go up to my room. Park there and be back down in a flash?"

"Just get the shit, Whitfield. Okay? I gotta be someplace."

Anything for my baby. I track Connor down in the lobby. He's with these two girls whom he intros as the Doublemint twins. The ones who were jumping rope in the seventies. Nice. Then I pull him aside. Unbelievable shit storm; he's out of goods. He's all, "Where were you at ten o'clock, jackass?" I explain I gotta keep Chelsea on my hook. He passes me some "X" compris, and words of wisdom to boot, "Roof the bitch."

By the time I crank out to the deck it's a mob scene. Agents, models, Kuwaiti bankers. But she's nowhere in sight. Figures, leave a hottie like Chelsea to these wolves she'll last negative five seconds. Fuck it, there's finies everywhere. I pop the roofies and grab on to one of the mattresses. There's a tangle of lithe young bodies. Tan legs and black sandals. I'm seein' double. The last thing I remember is this candle burning in some sea glass above my head, and then my lids come down. Crash.

ON-LINE INTERLUDE

MEMBER PROFILE

SCREEN NAME: MrPink40567
MEMBER NAME: Stu Bluminvitz
BIRTHDATE: 2/14/71
LOCATION: Paramount Commissary
MARITAL STATUS: Available—for now.
OCCUPATION: Independent Screenwriter
HOBBIES: Cons, big and small. Jewel heists. Protection rackets. Loan-sharking. Hits, for the right price.
PERSONAL QUOTE: "I don't tip."

MEMBER PROFILE

SCREEN NAME: Hottie47032
MEMBER NAME: Chelsea Starlot
BIRTHDATE: Old enough, barely
LOCATION: Over the rainbow
MARITAL STATUS: Waiting for you to make an honest woman of me.
OCCUPATION: Actress and making your HOTTEST dreams cum true.
HOBBIES: Dressing for you in my stiletto f**k me heels and grinding them into your back as you scream in agony.
PERSONAL QUOTE: I want you, I want to make you feel like a man and scream like a little girl.

Instant Message from MrPink40567
MRPINK: chelsea! its Stu!
HOTTIE: hi there, sexy man!
MRPINK: i was looking through the names and just saw your pro-file. must be fate huh? are you in the F 4 10" M room a lot?

HOTTIE: just waiting for you, big boy. ;)

MRPINK: wow. really? well, you are one hard gal to track down, i've been looking for you everywhere. didn't you get my msg?

HOTTIE: did you get the msg that I'm soooo hot and want you now?

MRPINK: no . . . you tried to call? i've been out a lot. i guess the pit bull forgot to tell me. but i got all your head shots posted!

HOTTIE: what r u wearin?

MRPINK: just my sneakers, jeans, partridge family t and baseball cap. and my new goatee, of course.

HOTTIE: you sound sexy. why don't you give it to me now?

MRPINK: ummmmm. . . . Ok. Gee, I'd almost got to thinkin that U were avoiding me.

HOTTIE: why? do you need to be spanked? ;>

MRPINK: not really. actually things have been goin great!

HOTTIE: my hair is soft and shiny from my Biogenetrix conditioner and i want you to cum all over it.

MRPINK: wow. well, that's a thought. you want to meet over at the Onyx for some coffee. they're having a comedy open mike and my friend joel is trying out some new material about the discovery channel.

HOTTIE: i want to beat you now and feel you explode all over my face.

MRPINK: i can see that. chelsea, this is so weird finding you. you know, my script is really taking off and I think there is a part now that would be perfect for you.

HOTTIE: how many inches is your perfect part?

MRPINK: it's the lead now. Yeah, we've had to make some changes. but you know me. i roll with the punches.

HOTTIE: do you roll with the spanks?

MRPINK: sometimes. ummmm, we got this great agent, todd hirtley, and he says it's a slam dunk. i'm sure i can push you for the part once the studio buys it. i know you'd be perfect.

HOTTIE: WHAT!?!!!!! What are you talking about?

MRPINK: yeah, i know you could just make this script.

HOTTIE: What is your script called, turdler?

MRPINK: kennel break, remember I told you about it at the formosa?

HOTTIE: and who the hell are you?

MRPINK: chelsea, itz stu . . . check my profile.

HOTTIE: JESUS H.! Who the hell told you to talk about this script?

MRPINK: what? it's my script.

HOTTIE: Wrong, dickbreath. It's your agent's script now! You do not touch it, do not cast it, DO NOT SPEAK ABOUT IT! EVER! Do you understand?

MRPINK: chelsea? what happened? why don't we meet at the onyx and talk about this?

HOTTIE: What did I just say shit boy? You do not talk. You do not leave your rathole. You do not speak to anyone until your agent gives you the green light.

MRPINK: you don't want to spank me anymore?

HOTTIE: If you open your mouth again I will see to it that the guards at the Writer's Guild open fire on sight if you ever try to register a single word again. I'm going to call Pac Bell and see about getting your phone turned off.

MRPINK: chelsea?

MRPINK: chelsea?

MRPINK: R U there?

MRPINK: :(

Six

Well, believe it or not, *Kennel Break* will be busting out at a theater near you any day now. However, until the big payday arrives, it looks like I am going to have to find a new job to tide me over. I might have been a little premature, moving out of my parents' place so soon, but when Mr. Whitfield got on board, I smelled a hit and was ready to take a few risks. But, with rent due in four days, and myself unemployed, I think I'll soon be applying for a loan from the First National Bank of Mr. and Mrs. Bluminvitz to keep me safely in the 323.

I could tell this was not going to be my day as soon as I got to work. I had hardly taken my seat behind the reception desk when Deana Cohen rushed in holding a stack of scripts three feet high. I said. "Good morning, Miss Cohen," and as she looked up her scripts and fell onto the floor, her triple-vanilla latte spilling all over them.

I picked the scripts up and dried them off while she told me what an idiot I am, a sign, maybe, that she was not appreciating my work. As I carried the scripts into her office, I tried again to talk with her about how I had incorporated her notes into *Kennel Break* without losing the integrity of the concept. "So, I did your notes," I said.

But she just looked up from her desk, held out her hand, and said, "Don't even." She still didn't realize what a gold mine she had working at her front desk.

The phones got pretty busy and amazingly enough, I answered a call for Deana from Mr. Whitfield. Once you're in the door, this town gets really small.

"Mr. Whitfield," I said. "It's Stu!"

He must have been coming off a pretty wild night because he didn't seem to recognize my name. "Stu, Stueeey, oh yeaiah!" he said a few times.

"Your writer! Your boy!" I reminded him.

"Stuminator! Ma boy! Whassup, my man!" He finally remembered. "Wait Stuey, watcha doin' at the Cohen palace, dee?"

"It's my temp job. I'm working here while I wait for my big royalty check." The Pit Bull says that it never hurts to remind the money people that you've got your eye on them and their wallets.

"Cool. Okay, my man. Now I need you to promise me you're going to swing low on this. Hirtley and I executing the major backfield play. Going for the Hail Mary, and you gotta sit tight. Don't let anyone know you're in our maneuvers. You're our secret agent man."

"You don't think I should try to take a meeting with Deana while I'm here?"

"No, no, no, no. Ma boy. Increase the peace. We're looking large for you. Keep the lips sealed and the eyes on the prize." I took his advice and sat quietly for the afternoon, even containing my excitement when I took a message for Deana from Tonya asking what she knew about Hirtley's dog script.

I was holding it all in but at 2:00 the dam burst when I answered a call from the man himself, Todd Hirtley. "Hirtley here for Cohen," he said.

"Todd!" I exploded. "It's Stu! Your client!"

"My what?" he asked.

"Your client. Author of the soon to be a major motion picture, *Kennel Break!*"

"What are *you* doing there?"

I explained to him about my temp work and told him we'd be sharing a table at Toscana soon enough.

"Listen, shithead," he responded. "I do not speak to clients in the middle of a spec sale. I've told you once to keep your mouth shut and never tell anyone you know me again. Now put Cohen on the phone." These high-flying superagents are a pretty super-stitious lot.

Despite all the buzz around town about my script, I managed to stay behind the desk and keep calm until 4:00 in the after-noon when Deana walked up and threw a script on my desk. "I need a copy of this now. And make it two-sided, loser," she said. I looked at the script and what do you know? It was my latest draft of *Kennel Break*.

When I brought the copy to her office, I just couldn't contain myself. With all the excitement about *KB*, I figured Deana would be pretty psyched to find out the author was none other than her very own temp.

"Deana," I said quietly. "I've got to tell you something. It's really important."

Without looking up from her desk she yelled, *"Get out! Now!"*

"Deana! Deana! Seriously, I'm Stu Bluminvitz! The author of *Kennel Break!*" I blurted.

"That's it! I can't work with you here!" She grabbed the phone, still not understanding. "Roger, please! We've got to fire this moron! It's him or me!"

I started to plead, but she was telling everyone to fire me. I took out my driver's license so she could see who I really am, but she wouldn't look, so I leaned over the desk to stick it in front of her eyes.

"Oh my God!" she screamed into the phone. "He's attacking me! He's totally wigging! Call security, quick!"

As I tried to explain, she kept screaming into the phone until suddenly these three huge studio security guys arrived, put me into a headlock, and dragged me down the hall by my hair. As everyone came out of their offices to see what the commotion was about, I cried, "It's my script! I swear!" But they couldn't make out my words over Deana's screaming that I was trying to kill her.

The security guard dragged me across the lot and threw me onto the sidewalk. Not the most auspicious way for a writer to leave a studio, I'll grant you. But the Pit Bull said that he has been banned from every lot in town and they always beg to get him back when they need him.

I had a really weird run-in on-line with Chelsea. It ended kind of badly, but she said enough to let me know that our relationship hasn't all been in my imagination. Chelsea Bluminvitz. Has a nice ring to it, doesn't it?

CHELSEA

This town is so 100 percent fucked that even frying in a Brunei harem would beat trying to get your career rolling here. (Where the fuck is Brunei anyway?) Not only has Jeffrey Dahmer, Jr. tracked down my liquor store, my dry cleaners, my hair salon, my Kinko's, and my manicurist, but I've got Tupac Schwartz, alias that shithead Whitfield, telling everyone at SkyBar, Bar Fly, Good Bar, and the rest of Sunset Strip that we are like engaged or something. *And* the queen of the jungle, Todd Hirtley, has his assistant calling me every half hour to make suggestions on what kind of conditioner I should use and what color panties to wear with a pink top.

And you might think that for all my many stalkers at least one of them would have enough balls to land me some kind of for-real acting job. But I suppose that would force the lard-asses to actually do some work instead of devoting their careers to phone-sex fantasies or whatever the *fuck* they call work.

I have a lot of anger toward this town right now and thank God Morton is there to help my deal with it. We had a major freakin' getting-clear session in class and it has helped me relax so much. I finally let him take me over to the Celebrity Center for the communications workshop. I swore not to join a cult but I mean, who fucking cares? I'll be a Scientologist. I'd become a fucking Hare Krishna, shave my head, and sell flowers at the airport if it could get me just one decent walk-on.

I didn't see any celebs at the center, but one of the sailors told me Juliette Lewis had just left. (She was amazing in *Natural Born Killers*. I can't believe she's a Scientologist.) I told them that if they even try to put in me in a sailor's suit they can forget washing my brain. But Morton was really cool about it and laughed.

Morton explained something about a Lord Zemu and how some guys he stuck in a cave a zillion years ago are poisoning my body, and I'm just like, yeah, yeah, get on with it already. So they tape all these electrodes to my arm, hooking me up to some kind of lie detector, and then ask me to talk about high school. I told them all the girls hated me, so what? And they asked why and I'm, like, because I was fucking hot, duh.

They asked me when I realized I was hot and I remembered the time in ninth grade when Bobby was all over me, trying to get me drunk and make it with me under the bleachers during a football game. Then I remembered how the principal found us and took me to his office and showed me his schlong and wanted me to touch it. And all this stuff started coming out about what is was like being the sole object of lust for a tiny Indiana town and how quickly you realize you can do so much better than all the dipshits who haunt you day and night, and how I grabbed the first Greyhound out to L.A. on my eighteenth birthday before I got knocked up with one of their little redneck babies.

Okay, I admit it was fucking wacko, but the whole thing made me feel a lot better, so who cares. It was like they were taking away my anger or something. Morton said they were removing the negative Thetans who had kept me from expressing myself. They told me I have a lot to be ashamed of but that they could help me stay focused. Whatever. He also gave me some pills and said I have to come back every three days. Who knows? Maybe it works.

I was still so completely fried from the brain burn during dinner with Jerry's nephew at Toi Thai. So when he mentioned he was going to the family's place in Aspen I said, I am so there, dude. He went for it and said okay.

That night, I got a call from Hirtley at 2:00 A.M. He was all pissy and says, "What business do you have in Aspen?"

I was just not in the mood and told him, "Look, screwhead, if you don't want this whole town to hear about your blue taffeta prom-dress fantasies, you better do a little less obsessing on my social life and a little more cranking on business. I want you lining me up some auditions, pronto, 'cause I have got every word of yours on tape."

He completely way wigged. "You're lying. You don't have any tapes."

I just said, "Buy me or try me. Later," and hung up.

We flew to Aspen and took a shuttle bus to the house that was this three-floor max-security log cabin. I had just parked in a room downstairs when a limo pulled up and the great studio boss Jerry himself walked through the house holding his head in his hands. He saw me sitting in the living room and without even introducing himself said, "If they call, I'm not here. If they knock, I'm not here. I'm not here." And he went straight upstairs, slamming the door of the master bedroom behind him.

That night, nephew said he was going to meet some Beverly

High buddies in town and asked if I wanted to come. Not. I get enough drunken Schwimmer look-alikes drooling on me at home, thanks all the same. So he split and I just soaked in the Jacuzzi on the deck, trying to get all these Hollywood ass-fucks out of my head and grateful that Jerry was locked in his room so I didn't have to deal.

I got to bed at about 10:00 but woke up at 3:00 in the morning. Nephew still wasn't back but as I lay in bed, I heard this terrible moaning from upstairs. At first, it sounded like bellowing laughter, and then was crying and then laughing again. I followed the noise upstairs to outside Jerry's door and the crying started again and I wondered if he was having a stroke or something. Then the laughing again and I couldn't take it so I knocked on the door but he didn't hear and the laughing or the seizure or whatever it was continued. So I open the door and there was Jerry sitting on the bed in his pinstriped boxers watching a Felix the Cat cartoon on TV, doubled over in laughter. He started crying again, like horrible sobbing and he looked up and saw me and said, "We don't make them like this anymore. Why not? I can't take it. Oh, God!"

And I'm all like, dude are you all right, but he's just crying. So I sat down on the bed and was like, "Get a grip. You own the world and shit."

And he said, "But they're after me. They all are." He told me how these like Japanese samurai or kamikazes or something are stalking and trying to kill him.

So I told him, "Dude, if you want to hear about stalkers, you have come to the right place."

We ended up talking. His nephew didn't come back until Sunday night, so I spent the weekend just lying around with Jerry, watching the Cartoon Network and making plans to fire his worthless VP's who do, like, zero work. We drafted a lot of really harsh "you're fired" letters to see who can write the meanest.

I'm feeling better now. I'm due at the center in half an hour, so gotta motivate. Jerry says he's going to find a part for me but at this point, I'll believe it when I see the credit sequence.

GRAND MASTER PRODS
Eric Whitfield, Commander-in-Chief

My man Hirtley is a work of poetry in progress. His moves are unbelievable. Todd-O has pulled the fine maneuvers that have this town jizzing themselves until there ain't nothing left to take home to mama. Hollywood wants *Kennel Break* like a schoolboy wants his first taste of honey and Grand Master Whitfield is right alongside, swinging from the ropes at the top rung.

Just check Hirtley's game plan: First he pulls his backdoor long run about not being able to take the enormous heat rising off this red-hot spec and planning to quit the business. Then he's got his boys at Neutron carrying side plays, spreading word that the script is the bomb, that it's already been sold, that it's going back for rewrites, that it's a small independent family film, that it's a big-budget actioner; anything that keeps the tracking machine on their toes falling all over themselves to step up to the plate for a piece of the Hirtley magic.

While the rumor machine is in full swing, Hirtley himself lays low, hiding out at home and fighting off desperate calls on his voice mail. Finally, after a full week, the Man reappears at the office and announces *Kennel Break* has entered final launch countdown. But this move he throws in is the killer: On Monday, he tells the town the script is going out on Tuesday. Then Tuesday A.M., he faxes out one line from the script to each target. That's it. One line. People without juice just get a slug line like EXT. QUIET SUBURBAN STREET—NIGHT. The big players get a line of dialogue. His good, good friends get action. I had to push for my boy Ertel at Aeroflux to get the line where Natasha pulls on her cat suit.

After the fax run, Hirtley phones up his contacts and lays it on the line, "You have all you need to know. If you want to see more, you make a bid." And they bite. As of this moment, the bidding war has climbed up to the middle six. And who should be at the center of this feeding frenzy: None other than Eric J. Whitfield, president of Grand Master Productions and owner of the *exculsivo* worldwide rights.

But this is just the beginning; the bidding war is just a prelude to a major showdown Hirtley's got planned. Now that he's already got some bids on the table, tomorrow he releases the full script citywide and goes nuclear.

After getting me to diss my D-Girl black book, telling them they've got no shot at *KB*, Todd's got me playing up to them, letting them think they might have just a small chance. I've been giving D-Girl land a taste of the Whitfield magic for the past week. Most of these gals I laid down with when I first got out to L.A., before I got plugged in with the primo hotties, so naturally the ladies have been dying for a return climb up Mount Whitfield ever since.

The one Hirtley tells me to really focus on is Deana Cohen, because he's got a massive hard-on to get in with Jerry. I know she's still wanting me because I ditched her at Kayla's birthday party a few years back when she got fucked-up and was clinging to my action like an angora sweater all night. So I call her up to make plans, and who is working the desk there but ma boy, Stu. He tells me his name but I can't place the face at first. But soon as I picture him, I go into panic mode as he pitches me to get himself into the game. Whoa, boy. Sit tight, I tell him. Whitfield's looking large for you. Like the poor stooge has anywhere else to go. He eats my shit up, though. The slob worships me and that will keep his lips zipped.

So I get the Deana on the phone and she is playing it supercool; she's afraid to get twice burned by the Whitfield flame. "What do you want, Whitfield?" she says. "I am super-busy."

"Dea-na. My woman. Where you been? I been looking high and low for you and you've left me hanging."

"I've been working, Whit-shit. Now get to the point."

"Okay, doll. I was wondering if I could take you to dinner. Maybe have some quality time to get caught up and reacquainted and all that fine stuff."

She is quiet, like dead calm, for about a minute. "What's your angle? What do you want?"

"Whoa, baby. Business is done for the day. The store is closed. I just wanted an up-close and personal with the hottest D-babe in town."

"*Pfft*. Whatever. Are you buying, because my credit card is beyond maxed out."

"You know it, sugarscript. Whitfield's giving you the full ride."

"Chaya? No, that's over. Vida."

"You got it, babe."

"Right. Meet me there at eight. And if I'm late, you better fucking wait for me."

"I've been waiting my whole life, doll."

"Whatever." And she hangs up, probably gushing with ecstasy, looking forward to her Whitfield evening.

She shows up at Vida an hour late. I had to slip the maître de a fifty to hold our table, but my cash spoke loud. Deana stumbles in, looking pissed off and disheveled with a pink butterfly hair clip barely hanging onto the bottom of one long, askew strand. As she shook her head back and forth, angrily looking for me, the butterfly clip flew around, slapping her on the sides of her neck. Each time it hit her she swatted at it, like a moth was buzzing around her. Finally, she found me and sat down, saying, "Can I just tell you? I have had the day from hell? Do you know what I mean?" She launched forthwith into a two-hour monologue about how many scripts she's got to read that night, how hard it is for her to be taken seriously in a man's business, her

asshole up-all-night neighbors, her stolen stereo, her incompe-
tent coworkers, her backstabbing friends, and some temp she
had to ax after he attacked her.

The pace of her monologue is fueled by the eight of Vida's
drink of the day, peppermint Schnapps with cranberry juice and
Augustino bitters. Man, the D-girl mating ritual of bludgeoning
your dude to submission with the extended play-by-play of your
day from hell gave this boy a major workout. But this was business. Grand Master Prods depended upon Deana knowing that
I was staying with her for every grunt.

Finally, after dessert she paused to shovel down a licorice
tiramisu and I got a chance to pull my move. "Baby, I hope in
your full-tension rush you're not missing out on the hottest spec
in town that's about to be snatched up from under you."

"I don't miss anything, jerk-off," she says.

"So you've stepped up to the plate on *Kennel Break?*"

"Hirtley's dog movie?"

"Hirtley's script from Grand Master Productions."

"What?"

"That's my script. I produced it," I tell her.

"Listen, Whitfield, the script is a really great concept and I
think with the right development it might be worth looking at
down the line someday, but Todd is so persona non fucking grata
with Jerry that I would have to be on way more drugs than you
can get to walk his name down the hall."

Now I make the big play. I touch her hand on her martini
glass, look deep into her bleary red eyes, and say, "You know,
Deana, it would be the fulfillment of a lifelong dream to be able
to get together with you on a hot project."

She looks back at me and sneers in that way D-girls do when
they're trying to be flirtatious and says, "Whatever. Do you have
Showtime?"

"I am hooked up to it all, babe."

"Great. This director I'm meeting with has his episode of *Red Shoe Diaries* on tonight and I need to watch it."

"Let me escort you to Casa Whitfield."

"Fine. But if you think I'm staying over, you are, like, completely high."

So I picked up the check and we split to my love nest. We get close on my black leather couch and I give her the old back massage while she watched her show. About fifteen minutes into it, she flipped it off and said, "This director has a style. I think we're going with him."

"Way to close the deal, babe."

"Whitfield, when it comes to visuals, I am the best there is." She sighs, throws back the Bombay martini I made her, and says, "So, did you want to kiss me or did you just invite me over to show off your Porsche posters." When it comes to business, I am a man of action and sprang to work posthaste.

She actually wasn't so bad. There is something kind of sexy about the way she refuses to lift a toenail to please a man. Afterwards, however, the hook sank in. As we were lying there, sprawled across my Persian floor rug, she suddenly says, "So are you going to tell Todd or should I?"

"Um, how do you mean, 'tell Todd,' baby?"

"Well, you knew when you asked me out that he and I are in a committed, serious relationship, right?"

"Knew? Uh, no, he never mentioned that little factoid."

"Well, we are. He probably didn't tell you because you're not high enough on the ladder for him to share his personal life with."

"Probably. So, baby, you going to share these details with him?"

"I don't know. Let's see what happens with the script." And with that, she pulled her clothes back on and bid Casa Whitfield a fond farewell.

THE NEUTRON AGENCY
Memo: #14485

0600 hours. We are down in the Neutron nail room. Get all this down, dick breath. History will want to study this moment. Plan. Preparation. Rehearsal. Surprise. Confusion. Purpose. Mission accomplished!

I have them wound tight as knots. Sixteen elite couriers, lined up end to end, shirts tucked, shorts pulled high.

"Gentlemen, you are the best of the best." I paid top dollar for these boys and they look good. "Today, each one of you represents a possible victory, a kill, a moment of pure strength. Gentlemen, a door to your future has been opened." This is what they've been waiting for. "The first one of you to arrive at his destination on the studio lot has a job in the Neutron mail room. Guaranteed. Anyone whom delivers the sale script, job in the mail room. Count on it.

"But, if anyone drops the ball, takes a wrong turn off Barham, or so much as stops for a two-ounce Cinnabon, I will personally see to it that your chapped ass is hand tossed from this county *in perpetuum*." Von Clausewitz writes that threats make far greater motivators than rewards.

"Demeanor. When you walk into a VP's office, you are an ambassador of this great agency. You walk brusquely and with purpose. If I get reports of meandering or messengers who looked lost, you are through. Do you hear me? Finished." That got to those little bastards.

"Johnson, you're going to Kevin Meyerson's office on the Universal lot—what gate do you enter from?"

He shuffles his white Reeboks over my sisel. "Uh, I don't know the number but it's, uhhh, the high rise."

I get in his face. "Do you mean the black tower, newt? Is that what you are trying to say?" He nods up and down. "That is gate number four. Learn it well!" Let's see, any last words for the troops. "It is exactly oh-six-thirty hours. You have until oh-seven hundred to complete your mission. War is an extension of politics by other means. Conventional methods of establishing this agency's primacy on the face of the entertainment infrastructure have failed. That is why we turn to you, our elite shock troops to take the front lines in the battle to determine whether Neutron shall be merely one of many or be remembered through the ages as the most effective integrated talent and literary agency of all time.

"Gentlemen, grab your scripts!"

And now my end. A few well-placed messages waiting on voice mail. Let's see. Start with that little tart, Deana. Jerry is a must. "Deana, Todd Hirtley. Here's the deal. I'm doing you a favor. Script going out today. You have it exclusive until oh-nine hundred. If I don't hear a *yes* from you by oh-eight-forty-five, you're off my list. For life."

Click. That always fires the little minxes up. Now, Schneider at Majestic. A comer's got to have the whole town on speed dial. "Shneides, Todd Hirtley. I'm going to make you a somebody today. Are you listening, boy? By the time you hear this there should be a script in your IN box. That's right, I'm giving you a shot at *Kennel Break*. Summer '98 B.O. king. Am I clear? Call me by oh-nine-hundred or you lose."

Guns loaded. Coordinates set. Need some goddamn Starbucks. Hair ball! Where's my latte? Set phones for pulse. Going to headset and war face. "Buttmunch, get me *Variety* on four. Now! What? Whitfield's on the line? Fuck him. All right, put him on speaker and take it all down."

"Hirtley here. You got eight seconds. Go."

"Todd, the master. My man."

"What do you want? I am trying to sell a script."

"Right. Okay, Mr. Big. I just wanted to update you on progress in D-Girl land."

"Any developments worthy of interrupting my schedule?"

"Well, my man, I closed the deal on Cohen; think we got a good inroad there."

"What do you mean, you closed the deal? Is she buying it?"

"Not that deal exactly, *el mucho hombre*. More like—"

"Like what?"

"Like the private, you know, personal deal. The thing is, I didn't know—"

"Whitfuck. Will you tell me what the hell you are talking about?"

"Right. Just getting to that, *jefe*. So you know how it goes with the minxes and in the end, I laid down with her."

"On the script?"

"Not exactly. More like, on the bed. On the floor, precisely."

"You're telling me you fucked her?"

"That's it, my man. I'm sorry."

"Shithead?"

"Right here, Todd-O."

"Why are you bothering me with this?"

"Well, I just thought you'd want to hear from me first. The thing about it all is that I had not a clue that you and she were, like, on the road to loveland together."

"Where did you get that idea? The only road Deana and I are on together is the red carpet to Jerry's office."

"What? Well, I just thought—"

"You think I would touch that cow?"

"Whoa, my man, have you gotten a close-up of her lately? She's looking fine."

"She is a nothing."

"I don't know about that, Todd. She's coming up in the world too. The gal's got a lot of people talking."

"Whitfuck, get off my phone line. When I want to talk to you I'll let you know. Shitboy, disconnect him."

What the fuck was that about? Hmm. An interesting digression. Is it true that Cohen is now considered viable? Look into it, shitboy. Perhaps I've been hasty.

Okay. Move! I want *Variety* on the line yesterday!

DEANA

Can I just warn you guys? Eric Whitfield is literally the worst sex you will ever have in your entire lives. I mean, for all the bravado about his "moves on the la-dies," his idea of, like, pleasing a woman is like ten minutes of dry humping before giving himself a huge high-five and "all right!" and calling it a night. I don't think he's gay though; he's just still a frat boy. Normally I would have never done dinner in the same universe as him, but I was totally pissed at Todd for not calling me back so I said, Whitfield's kind of cute and he's buying, so what the fuck.

Todd has been sulking lately because I refuse to so much as mention his name to Jerry. I've explained to him a thousand times that it's not that I don't really love him, I've just got to make my career the top priority and not let my personal life cloud my judgement. Do you know what I mean? It's not like I didn't turn his script around by giving him the notes to make it a women's movie in the first place. And it's not like every other studio isn't bidding on it. But I guess Mr. Power Ranger is feeling a little hurt that I don't want to play with him. It's kind of cute to see him like that. After work today, I'm stopping at Barneys and buying him the powder blue bathrobe with the fluffy collar I saw him checking out last week.

Work has been so much better since I got rid of that psycho temp. Can you even believe he actually attacked me? Next time I get a day off, I am without a doubt filing a restraining order against him. Our new temp is a Billy Crudup look-alike who handles the desk like a pro. Life is literally a million times better with him on the phones.

I had the worst meeting ever this afternoon. I've been developing this, like, Latino family drama meets Antonio Banderas action script with this writer, Carlos, for the last eight months, but everyone at the trackers' dinner last night at Newsroom was saying that Hispanic is, like, way, way over and that Asian is the new big thing. So I had to tell Carlos that unless he can prove he can write Asian and redo the script in a week, I've got to pull him off the project and get a Chinese boy. Of course, he totally cried. Writers are so predictable.

Whoa, I am seriously late for my pedicure. Gotta run.

JERRY

(Tape begins)
Hello? *Hellooooo?* Are you on? Cheryl, it's happening again! Right, right, right. Just talk. Yes, I fucking knew that. Whadya think, Hotatsi hires imbeciles to run their studio? Ha!

Here I am again, dealing with my anger. Fantastic damn way to kill time when one of Hollywood's great film studios is crumbling around my feet. Stupid fucking Dr. Birnbaum says my blood pressure has gotten so high, even with the pills, that it's still at a level that can't support human life. So why don't they just make stronger fucking pills? Doesn't take Oppenheimer to figure out that! But no, they want to keep me in pain, get me hooked on their worthless pills and valves and monitors for the rest of my life. Goddamn parasites. I ought to show them how to meet a bottom line every day. Every now and then it helps to cure someone, have a satisfied customer to great good word of mouth. Maybe I'll go into the drug business after I bail out of here.

But the fucking anger is getting under goddamn control. Fired all my VP's last weekend and I am feeling a whole fucking lot better not having to look at their pathetic faces. At this morning's staff meeting it was just me which was perfect. The firings made the Japs happy. Showed them I am taking charge of the situation. Boosted the stock price. I'm not going to hire any replacements for the time being. Postpone having to look at a whole new crew of fuckups.

If only Chelsea could be a VP. Go-getter like her could run this company better than a thousand blood-sucking Ivy MBA's. Should I try it? Naw. The Japs would never swallow that one. Got to find a part for her. Make her star who can bring back this studio like Alicia Silverstone was going to do for Sony. She's been taking me for kickboxing lessons at this Crunch joint down in fagelatown. Great stuff. Working out a lot of anger. Feeling better. Keep my eyes open for a project for her.

Ah, I remember the days when I was a producer. I could find a hotshot young writer and director, follow my gut, and make some movies. Now, I just sit in this office letting the town tear me apart, bite by bite, while my employees slowly burn this studio to the ground and the Japs try to corner me, demanding some answers about when we are going to turn things around here. *When someone in this town gets off their tuchus and brings me a decent idea we can turn into a vertically fucking integrated entertainment product.* That's when. I've managed to dodge them for three months now but they've been carpet bombing me with memos, trying to get hold of me. They want me to come to Tokyo and explain to the fucking board. *Variety* reported today that they've hired Anthony Pellicano to find me. Damned traitor, after all the business I've sent his way. Jesus fucking Christ on a crutch, what is there to explain—that they've sunk their money into a worthless can't-do sinkhole in the city that always sleeps; that they would've gotten a better return on their investment building a bonfire out of the money and selling marshmallows alongside? And this is my fault? Christ already.

Take a look at this tracking report. Let's see what's out there—

serial killer, serial killer, romantic comedy. That'll turn things around, throw some money after another sitcom star, spend eighty million to find out that Miss Prime Time Perky can't open a picture. A disaster movie—how about the story of this studio if they want to see a disaster? Ha! Holy shit, a Western? I'm paying these people to read Westerns? Have they bought a time machine to send the audiences back to 1935 with them? Drama about a coal miner's strike. I don't need an Oscar, I need a hit.

Wait a second. Hold on. What the fuck is this? *Kennel Break?* A dog-heist women's film. Have I been talking to my fucking self for the last three years? There's an animal-action script on the lot and no one tells me? Great Caesar's ghost, that little brat Cohen has been sitting on this? What the fuck is going on here?

Cheryl! I want Deana Cohen and her dog script in here yesterday! Tell them to run. Bring a group in. Put together a reading for me. Assign everyone characters.

I'm getting that old feeling again. In my bones. This studio is about to make the turnaround of the century. Look out Morton's! Put away your daggers, Jerry is back!

Cheryl! How do I turn this thing off!

From *KENNEL BREAK*
Notes by JERRY

EXT. GENEVA VETERINARY CLINIC—NIGHT.

ANGLE

Across the palatial grounds of the clinic. From inside the mansion, the sounds of a festive BLACK TIE party are heard.

(NOTE: What is this black-tie crap doing in a kids' movie?)

Suddenly, four female figures in BLACK LEATHER CAT-SUITS and ski masks SLINK across the lawn.

A lone guard approaches and rushes them, wielding a GUN.

Natasha steps forward and KICKS the GUN out of his hand. With another swift KICK in the jaw, the guard hits the floor.

(NOTE: Fuck the karate and get the dog in here already.)

> NATASHA
> *(to the Guard)*
> Ready for some more.

He lies motionless on the ground.

> NATASHA
> Just like my ex. Never could get it up for a second round.

(NOTE: PG!!!!!!!!)

The girls laugh.

> FREDO
> So what are you going to do with your share of the diamonds?

> NATASHA
> By the time this job is over, I am going to need the pedicure of a lifetime.

CHARLENE

Well, girls. You'll be able to find me in St. Tropez with a very special cabana boy you all remember.

(NOTE: What the fuck?)

ALL

Do we ever!

NATASHA

Make sure he gives you the full-body treatment.

(NOTE: Are you people out of your minds?)

FREDO

But don't forget the coconut oil.

They all giggle.

(NOTE: What the hell is going on here? You're talking about *schtupping* the pool boy in a kids' movie? Get fucking rid of all this. No *Friends*, just Natasha and a dog!)

NATASHA

Come on, girls. We've got work to do. We can't cash in those diamonds until we find our little Scooby.

They pull off their catsuits and reveal full SATIN EVENING GOWNS underneath.

(NOTE: Where is the fucking dinosaur?)

From *Daily Variety*, July 24, 1997
HOTATSI HOTSY-TOTSY FOR CANINE CAPER
By Dan Dempsy

In what is possibly the largest purchase price ever for a spec script by a first-time writer, Hotatsi Pictures has paid a reported 1.7 million dollar, for writer Sy Blumsky's *Kennel Break*. The script focuses on a young woman's fight to save her Dalmatian from a series of sinister monsters created by a mad scientist.

A Hotatsi spokesman labeled the script, "one of the finest animal adventures Hollywood has ever seen. We are thrilled to be planning our summer campaign around *Kennel Break*." Privately, studio sources tell *Variety* that the script will require a page-one rewrite to be completed "yesterday" if the project is to begin shooting in time for summer '98 release.

Kennel Break was the subject of a frenzied bidding war said to involve at least four major studios. According to Neutron Agency's Todd Hirtley, who repped the sale, "the excitement over this script shows the unstoppable firepower behind Neutron products." The bidding war over *Kennel Break* grew so heated that Hirtley abandoned his desk for three days last week in the midst of the feeding frenzy. "I needed some personal time for soul-searching before I could unleash the spec equivalent of the Ark of the Covenant upon the world," Hirtley says.

The script was shepherded through a troubled adolescence by Eric Whitfield of Kilimanjaro Productions who purchased an exclusive option to the script in April and becomes executive producer of the project. "I had to steer my boy through some rocky white waters, oh yeaih!" says Whitfield.

The purchase also represents a personal triumph for Hotatsi president Jerry Schnapper, who has presided over a string of box-office flops during his tenure at the helm and endured criticism for failing to set up a major project in over two years. Jerry's status on the lot reportedly became so tense in recent weeks that Tokyo-based Hotatsi executives hired famed Hollywood PI Anthony Pellicano to capture Schnapper and deliver him to Tokyo. "Reports of my disappearance were greatly exaggerated," said Schnapper in a *Variety* interview. "They couldn't find me because I was at work making the deal of a lifetime. And the folks at Hotatsi didn't get to be worth billions by not knowing that animals sell."

No talent or director has yet been attached to the project.

Seven

Roll Out the Barrel

ERIC WHITFIELD
and
KILIMANJARO PRODUCTIONS
Cordially invite you to
GET DOWN
and funky
In celebration of
the record-breaking spec sale
Kennel Break
Bud's—Thurs., August 19
10 P.M.

The Kilimanjaro Express is plowing forward full steam, rolling large and making no stops till the top o' Mount Olympus when we get groovy with the Gods! Oh yeah, boy!

Kennel Break's sale and my subsequent impressarial duties have guaranteed that Eric Whitfield Productions will be the stuff of party legend for decades to come. The spec-sale fiesta went seamlessly, cruising me to the highest possible A-list plus status at every rope in 213 and 310. I did it all by following the Tony Montana guidebook. First I got the cash—selling my script. Then I get the power—become the ultimate host and social arbiter with the sale party. Check. Now, I get the *pun-tang*. On top of the world, looking down on creation, yeah, boy!

Before I could guarantee the success of my party, I had to ensure the attendees would be desirables only. Which meant getting my uncombed goateed writer Stu as far from the festivities as possible. My boy is genius at the keypad, but though I love him like a brothah, the stooge ain't equipped to mingle big-league. What's more, I didn't want the lad hanging around trying to snatch up credit for this *coup de spec*. So when I learned that my friend Faisal's parents are spending August in St. Tropez, I finagled the keys to their villa in Puerto Villarta and handed Stuey two first-class tickets. He needs some space to plug in Jerry's notes on the script, I tell him. You should have seen the look on his face when I forked over the tickets. Such gratitude was truly inspiring. He cried, "First class! First class!" over and over. I don't think the fool has ever been on a plane before.

I made up the primo celebratory list for the party. I spared no one—the top agents, execs, producers, talent in town. I work Morton's, couldn't get a dinner reserve Monday night, but hung by the valet line with ticket in hand, like I was just leaving. As all the top names leave, I leaned into them and say to, for instance, Michele Pfeiffer, "Jerry said he's looking forward to seeing you Thursday." And when she asked where, I just told her, "it's on your calendar, don't worry." Before her car hits Melrose, I can see her on her cell bawling out her assistant for not passing along the invite. Then Lorenzo di Bonaventura arrives, and I tell him, "You just missed 'Chelle. She asked me to tell you that she's looking forward to seeing you at Bud's on Thursday." And then—get this—before he can get a word in, I walk away. Turn my back on him. *Cajones de steel*. That's what you need in this business, my man.

With the A-list notified, I worked the scene—SkyBar, Bar Marmont, Barfly, Grand Havana, the Gem, letting all the finies know where the players will be found. Discreetly passing out invites. Some of them want cash guaranteed before they will agree to show, but I'm just like, babe, it's not that kind of party. You're going to be paying me to get past the rope. I'm taking their names and numbers, putting them on my permanent list. And now who's got the hottest black book in town? Oh, yeah.

With the talent and the tail secured, I got cracking on the decor. We tent the parking lot and get Faisal's cousin Maxim, the hottest hip-hop/house DJ in town, to spin the killer tunes. The men with the big balls don't want to dance, but all the hotties will be on the floor keeping the scene juiced. In the back room, I set up a buffet and hired eight Crazy Girls strippers to dance, providing gratis lap service to my guests. But the front room is the coup de grâs. I upgraded Bud's classic cigar-lounge decor and set up a quiet deal-making facility for the players to do their work: faxes, E-mail access, the whole conference-facility 90 yards. I modeled the look on the LAX Ambassador Lounge. Money never sleeps, but it does party!

On the big night, I wound up escorting the Cohenator. I'm starting to get used to the gal. She's got this kind of sexy-slash-bitchy thing going down. What's more, she's flying high now from bringing in the *Break* and owes it all to Eric the Whit, another favor to call in down the line. She celebrated big-time at the party and got a little fucked-up and started stalking Hirtley, who doesn't even remember her name of late.

I cruised the room, checking the door to make sure none of the high rollers got the shaft, getting funky with the finies on the floor, pop in the back room for a quick lap dance and some fried zucchini and bacon hors d'oeuvres.

Had some trouble with the college crew. I flew out my investors to join the action, to see firsthand how their homey fares. Somehow, they read about the sale in the on-line version of the trades and had been howling for a piece of the purchase price. I tried to explain that this is not the time to take capital out, it's the time to keep the cash lines flowing, to throw good money after good. But they were giving me trouble so I invited them out, figure I'd give them a taste of the scene to keep them quiet.

Once the fools arrive, though, they go into the deal room and start a quarters game. I tell them, guys, this is big-time shit here and the frat antics are majorly tired. Then they move it to the back and start putting the moves on skirts that are way, way far out of their league. I even catch one of them pulling the block on Mike De Luca! Friends are friends and I love my homeys, especially when they're paying the bills, but when business is at hand, this man is an island. I tell the door guys to remove them pronto. As they're dragged off, one of them shouts, "You are gone, you bitch Whitfield! We paid for this party!" Who needs them anymore? With this *KB* score and the success of this part, I've got investors lining up around the block to get a piece of me. Anyway, my boys were out and the festivities continued uninterrupted. Every major hombre faces his moment when he must lock away his past and this first taste of the big time was my moment of truth.

By the end of the night, every major player in town had slipped me his card for permanent inclusion on the Kilimanjaro directory. I left early (got that move from *The Great Gatsby*, ditching your own party. The classics have all the moves!) and took the Deana home. She is so gassed from her up-and-comingness and enthralled by my mastery of the Hollywood machine that she gives me skull in the car outside my apartment. Let her enjoy it while she can, because it's not for long that I'm chilling in the back seat with D-girls. This train is rolling to the stars! Yeah, boy!

DEANA

You guys are not going to believe it. Can you say "Vice President Cohen?" Yes, way. Way way. As of this morning, I am officially the vice president for production development of one of the hugest studios in the entire world.

Just before we bought *Kennel Break*, Jerry had instituted this total, like, full-on VP housecleaning, getting rid of all the fuck-ups who had kept us in the basement for so long. And that housecleaning included my boss Roger, who I totally love for all the support he has given me, but I have to admit he was not up to giving Jerry what he needed. So after *KB* got set up as the major project that is going to hit, like, all-time box-office records worldwide, Jerry shopped around for a new VP and who else should he turn to but the woman who made the deal happen. You guys, I'm going to be so busy over the next few months over-seeing the development and production, but I swear, I am always totally there for you. Just call my new assistant and we can set up a lunch anytime. If you give me a couple of weeks notice.

But the humongous responsibility has already begun. The first project I look at this morning, after moving into my new corner office, is this thriller pitch the studio bought back in May from Adam Groschek, the *Friends* writer. It's been in constant development since then. We've had him do about a hundred drafts. But I'm looking at all the projects that I am in charge of and I'm all, like, no wonder we can't get anything going. We have a comedy writer working on a thriller.

So I call Groschek in for a meeting and I'm all, like, "Look, I know you're totally a great writer and all that"—it pays to stroke talents' egos—"But this is not your genre. So, I am totally sorry but we're going to have to give this script to Rick Drain." I thought I'd throw Todd a bone. After all, what is power for if you can't use it to help your friends.

But of course, Groschek got all defensive and pissy and started whining that the script is his idea, that this is the script he's always dreamed of writing. Yeah, yeah, yeah, just take a look at your contract and see who owns *your* idea.

I told him, "When you own a studio or become a VP of production development then you can write your dream script or do whatever lame-ass thing you want. But while I'm in charge here, it's up to me to make the call. You were on *Friends*. You are a comedy writer and nobody in this town is going to let you work out of your genre."

He gets all huffy and says, "I did one spec for *Friends!* What is this genre shit? Writers don't have genres, just ideas. What genre was Shakespeare? What genre was Dostoyevsky?"

"*Duhhhh*, their genre was classics. And yours is comedy. So I really appreciate your time, but I'm like a VP and have better things to do then sit around having literary debates with out-of-work writers." And I threw him out. Man, they never give you a break. The higher you get, the bigger the hassles.

Speaking of which, I am beginning to think Todd might have some major intimacy issues. I mean, after we set up *KB* it was so obvious what a great team we make, but I can't get him on the phone now. I thought he would take me to Whitfield's party and we could make the grand entrance together, but I couldn't get hold of him. I think he must know that our relationship is entering the serious stage and getting a little scared.

So I let Whitfield take me over to Bud's, figure I'll give him a treat for shepherding *KB* along. We walk in and every nobody tracker, my former peer group before the promotion, is immediately all over me, asking what projects are we setting up, have I read this script? What do I hear about that one? Who is going to take my old job? And I am totally surrounded, like the Beatles getting ripped apart by fans or something. So I'm just, like, "*Whoa! Losers!* I am not part of your little tracker games any more. I am a VP and if you want to talk to me you can call my assistant!" Thank God I'm rid of them. But don't worry. You guys are totally different, I'm *always* there for you.

Then who should I see Todd walk in with but this bimbo actress who's been hanging around Jerry's office lately. And I'm like so sure that she's really what you need, Todd. I'm sure your parents would love you to bring *her* back to the Maidstone Club. But I let him have his fantasies because it was so clear that she was not even acknowledging she was there with him. Halfway through the party, she snuck out with the DJ.

I hung out for a couple hours and let everyone congratulate me. It's great when people like me who have worked so hard for their success finally make it because it's an example to all the lazy wanna-bes that the only way to the top in this town is to earn it. I think everyone there really appreciated that I deserve all the success I get and were totally happy for me.

At about 11:00 I remember that I want to show up at the office by 6:00 tomorrow morning and get to the gym first, so I tell Whitfield to take me home. I'm all about setting priorities.

He says, "Ba-bie. You can't walk out now on the most high-powered locale in the universe."

And I'm like, "Whitfield, I don't care who they are. I am a VP. They can all just call my office."

THE NEUTRON AGENCY
Memo: # 14502

Well, shitboy, looks like my throne is going to be so big that there might even be room for your sorry ass on my lap. That's right, fuckup, I might— I repeat, *might*—finally be ready to get you a desk. As I am becoming a full partner, I could use a piss-boy working as a junior agent, serving as my eyes and ears amongst the lower echelons. Start scouting for open office space. Your time may come soon. But do not forget—everything you have is thanks to Todd Hirtley. And as Hirtley makes, so can he break. Did you get that down?

Some weird circumstance in the air at the victory soiree last night. First, I get the call from Jerry asking me to escort that Chelsea snatch to the party. He says "Hirtley, what time you going to that ridiculous fucking shinding I'm supposed to show my face at?"

I said, "Nine o'clock, sir."

He said, "Make it eight and pick up Chelsea on the way. Gotta bring my lousy wife."

I tried to tell him that I have plans to go stag with his nephew, so I can focus on business but he said, "My what? Nephew? You better get it together, Hirtley, or I'll bust your chops so hard you'll be sipping your fruity mango smoothies through a head brace. Chelsea will be ready at eight. Don't make her wait."

I tried to get in a little business in while I had him on the line.

"Sir, I just want you to know what a pleasure it is speaking with you and if you have a second to look at Rick Drain's rewrite I could . . ."

I heard a muffled sound on the other end, as though he were putting the phone down. Then I heard his voice in the background yelling, "*Cheryl! Cheryl!* This lousy phone is still talking. I'm done with my call and it's still talking! What's wrong with this thing?" And then the line went dead.

He was asking me to beard for him, wasn't he? Why does he think I should beard? Has he heard something? Find out. And what the hell is going on with him and Chelsea? This is not normal. I want to know what sinister forces are at work. Get on it.

I would have found out from the little slut herself if she had not transformed into the sister from another planet. I picked her up at her place on Laurel, down the street from the Virgin Megastore. When I knocked, she took a full fifteen minutes to answer, leaving me standing on the curb. She finally emerged, coked to the gills. The entire ride over she chattered two-thousand miles a minute, rubbing at her nose like she's trying to tear it off. When I ask her if she wants a back rub to calm her down before we went into Bud's, she said, "Your hands are polluted, Hirtley. If they come near me ever again, you'll hear from my attorney." Since when does she have an attorney?

Stranger still is her under-the-breath muttering about her childhood, anger, God knows what kind of insane shit is pouring out of her mouth. The whole drive she drivels, "It's not me. It's you. I am not the problem. I am not leaving. My body is pure. I am a temple of the gods."

Very strange, shitboy. Very strange.

We got to the party and Chelsea made a beeline for the bathroom. Despite the detour, I was in top form all night. Everyone wants a piece of me. This town is mine. The thrill of victory is, however, not untinged by sadness. I feel like Alexander the Great when he realized there was no piece of the world left unconquered and cried for days. What heights of Hollywood has Hirtley left unclimbed? Find out and make a list for me. Tomorrow we start work on a new five-year plan.

That little bitch Cohen was hanging on me like a cheap suit all night. Completely wasted, at one point she pulls me aside and tells me, "Todd, if only we could just cut through the denial so you could see how, like, totally afraid of intimacy you are."

What the fuck does she mean by that? I am not afraid of intimacy. I have every intention of having a perfect marriage and raising a world-class family as soon as work quiets down. I think my parents know I'm not afraid of intimacy. Don't I come back to Chicago for six days every Christmas? Am I not still my class leader for the Penn alumni association, keeping up my old contacts? Perhaps my romantic unavailability is beginning to raise eyebrows. Ask around, quietly. Make it look like you are snooping behind my back. And note to include wife and family on the five-year plan.

Chelsea spends the entire night in a coke-fueled dance fever and Jerry's nephew gets a hundred lap dances in the back room while I am cornered by the Cohen bitch.

Finally Jerry comes over and saves me, making the night worthwhile. He says, "What the fuck did you do with Chelsea?"

"She's out on the dance floor, sir. I am sure she would be delighted—"

"All right, shut up already!" Jerry puts his face right into mine and says, "You stay away from me, Hirtley!"

He storms off before I can thank him. Ah, women. How they can distract a man. Still, I think the channels of communication between Jerry and me have been opened and great things will come from our association. Fasten your seat belts, turdler, we are on the rocket jet to the top!

CHELSEA

Getting clear is so fucking rad. I can't believe I resisted for so long. At the center they are literally tearing me a new spiritual asshole, working me out with the technology, going back through my childhood, deeper and deeper into my issues. I can feel the psychic toxins oozing out of my body as I become pure like a goddess. There is no fucking way, however, in this or any other life, that I could face these memories without massive amounts of drugs to pull me through the ordeal. The Scientologists say that I have to keep myself pure and rely on the technology and the vitamins they sell me (on credit, ha!), but I am not even close to ready to start facing life spiritualized without a little bump to get me through when I'm sitting in traffic on the 405 and these third grade baby-sitter nightmares start rushing back. But as soon as I make it to advanced Thetan stage or whatever they call it, I am definitely going to taper off.

I am really worried about Jerry. His anger issues are making his life so hard and not one person at that studio can relate to what he is going through. I've been taking him kickboxing and spinning to channel his aggression and it seems to be helping. I talked him into cutting work one day and going to Magic Mountain. He called ahead to the park manager and got them to shut down the Batman ride so we could go on it over and over by ourselves. It was really satisfying seeing Jerry hanging from the Bat machine, flying around and around in circles, negative energy fleeing his body. I felt I was really doing the world some good. Morton wants me to bring him to the center, but I don't think he is ready yet.

While Jerry's big new movie is still in pre, I've been spending a lot of time at his office, helping him keep the studio on track. Mostly we've had to fire a ton of people and write some really fucking nasty memos. That definitely helps get rid of the tension.

Jerry had Hirtley take me to Whitfield's lame-o sale party, so he could bring his wife along. I could deal with riding in the car with Todd, but when he tried to maul me in the parking lot, I was just, like, sure, I believe you believe you want to fuck me.

The party was the same ridiculous Eurotrash starfucking loserville that has been trying to rub themselves against my boobs ever since I got off the Greyhound. It shows me how fucked up I was that I actually put up with these prickless wanna-bes for so long. But I have too much respect for myself and my spiritual growth now to let these creeps into my neighborhood anymore. After fighting off about a thousand of them, one of Whitshit's friends actually asked me for a lap dance. At that point, I realized I was completely out of coke. I talked Maxim the DJ, who has been the main supplier of the Strip for years, into putting on a long-playing tape and taking me back to his place.

We stayed up all night at his apartment in the Wilshire Corridor doing coke off a giant mirror on the floor. He was so fueled that he grabbed at me all night, but was too wasted to get serious about it. Finally at 4:00 A.M., I give him a blow job just to quiet him down and get his filthy hands off of me. At 7:00, he gave me cab fare and I split. It's 10:00 now and I'm due at the center in an hour and I'm feeling like shit crashing into the worst hangover of my life. I'm hurting, every inch of my body including my hair and toenails. I can hear my upstairs neighbors walking around their apartment and the sound of their feet pounding against my ceiling is so loud I feel like they are marching on my brain. If they don't settle down and sit still I am going to break into their place with my meat cleaver. I took a whole bottle of those Scientology vitamins but they haven't helped. Maybe Maxim is still up and can messenger me some more before my session.

USS BLUMINVITZ
CAPTAIN'S LOG
STARDATE 970918

Mexico certainly was an adventure. Working on this script I am beginning to feel a bit like John Huston in *White Hunter, Black Heart,* up the river filming *The African Queen* under savage conditions while trying to shoot an elephant with my trusty native guide and a bunch of insensitive Hollywood bureaucrats. That about sums up the experience so far.

Mr. Whitfield really took great care of me. That's how he got where he is today, knowing how to look after the talent, and there can be no more doubt that I am talent. He actually gave me two *first-class* tickets to Puerto Villarta. I think he meant the second ticket to be for a girl, but I knew how much it would mean to the Pit Bull to get back in the game and go on a real, exclusive Hollywood script retreat, so I brought him instead of inviting Chelsea. The last thing I needed under this pressure was a broad distracting me anyway. In fact, I secretly hoped that being around the process might get the Pit Bull to turn out his final masterpiece old-school script, or at least some tell-all memoirs. I think he was really excited when I broke the news to him, but he just said, "P.V. . . . got my jaw busted there once." Love him or hate him, the Pit Bull is a classic.

We got down to Mexico and our house turned out to be an enormous hacienda overlooking the bay. There were three live-in servants on hand to wait on the two of us around the clock. I had a lot of work to do, so I immediately hit the laptop while the Pit Bull took a stroll in town.

I managed to make most of the changes that Jerry wanted, but I must say, in my humble opinion, the direction of the script has fallen off the deep end. My Tarantino homage with a light touch is now the story of a female James Bond bonding with her baby dinosaur. Reading the notes, I almost considered taking my name off the project, but then I remembered that if this turns out to be one-tenth the hit that Mr. Whitfield thinks it will be, I'll be able to write my own ticket. Who knows? Maybe Quentin and I will collaborate on my next project and then we'll get it right.

It took me three days working around the clock to do all of their notes and basically rewrite the script from scratch. Thank God I finished it when I did because at 2:00 A.M. on the final day, the Pit Bull burst into the hacienda with fifty locals he picked up in town. Apparently when the bar closed, the Pit Bull remembered the wine cellar in the basement and invited his drinking buddies over to sample the wares. I tried to stop them, but a lone writer standing in front of a non–English-speaking drunken mob doesn't seem to have much of an effect. So I spent the next few hours trying to contain the damage and repairing the cellar door that they tore off its hinges.

For a little while things seemed to be more or less under control. But just as the sun was rising and the wine was almost gone, the Pit Bull looked across the room at one of the locals and yelled, "My God! Ratsbreath Murphy!"

"Yup, you found me Bull," the local replied.

As it turned out, this guy was another huge, enormous screenwriter and Howard Hawks collaborator in the fifties who had left town under mysterious circumstances way back when and had not been seen or heard from since. As it also turned out, when he disappeared he left the Pit Bull holding an IOU for a thousand dollars and took his girlfriend along for good measure.

Well, you know how these hard-drinking double-fisted writers are about grudges—they never forget them. It couldn't have been more than two seconds after he had ascertained Ratsbreath's identity that the Pit Bull leapt across the room, tackled him to the floor and proceeded to strangle the life out of him.

As it also turned out, old Ratsbreath seemed to have become a rather popular figure during his stay in Puerto Villarta, because the locals seemed none too happy to just stand by and watch him throttled to death on the living-room floor. They decided to correct this by pulling the Pit Bull off and tearing him almost limb from limb. Then, not content with mere bloodshed, the mob decided to have a go at the house as well. I don't know how it all got so out of hand, but the last thing I remember before the police showed up was a king-sized poster bed falling off the balcony into the ocean.

The police put the Pit Bull and me in our own cell and booked us for inciting a riot. They gave me one phone call, so I placed it collect to Mr. Whitfield. I think I woke him up.

"Kizzamanjarhead prods," he answered.

"Mr. Whitfield. It's Stu!" I yelled into phone.

"Stu, my man. It's okay, the party's over now. You can come back, homeslice."

"Actually, Mr. Whitfield, I can't. I'm in a Mexican jail."

"Yeah, boy! Whacha doin' there, Dee?

I explained to him about the house. He seemed pretty upset, but kept thinking straight, like a pro.

"Stu, my boy. This is not good. Where is the rewrite? I got to have it in tomorrow."

"That's safe. When the trouble started I hid my laptop in my bedroom-ceiling tiles, just like in—"

"Okay, my boy. Your pimp daddy's got it under control. I'm going to send a courier down to go fetch your computer and bring it home. And then I'll explain to Faisal that we will pay his parents back out of your share."

"Fair enough. But, Mr. Whitfield, will the courier be able to bail me out?"

"Stuey, I think you are mistaking me for someone with much larger clout than I got. I don't have the kind of muscle to pull you out of a Mexican jail."

"But he just needs to bring down the bail money—"

"My boy, my wad's wrapped so tight now I don't think I can front you that kind of change—"

"Can you call a lawyer?"

"Sit tight. They'll let you out soon enough. I got to get movin' if I'm going to rescue that script. I'm always thinking of our future. Whitfield's lookin' large for you."

And he hung up. I guess it was good news that the script would be taken care of and that Faisal's, parents would be okay, but that wasn't really what I was thinking of while stuck in the cell with a bleeding Pit Bull and three angry Mexican drunks who were starting to give me some very strange, hungry looks.

A day later, when they let me have another call, I broke down and called the powers that be: Mr. and Mrs. Bluminvitz. They agreed to send a lawyer to bail me out, but were not quite understanding about this turn in their son's career. I tried to explain to them that even this might work out for the best; I heard that Kevin Williamson is thinking about doing a Mexican prison film and might just be looking for a writer.

Eight

HOTATSI PICTURES
PRESS RELEASE

FOR IMMEDIATE RELEASE

Hotatsi Pictures has completed preproduction work on next summer's blockbuster *Kennel Break*, the story of a glamorous, international woman of mystery who teams up with a baby Tyrannosaurus rex to stop a team of dog smugglers. Says Hotatsi chairman Jerry Schnapper, "This picture is going to be the blockbuster to break all blockbusters. A good-time shoot-'em-up with lots of cuddly animals and a terrific knockout heroine."

Hotatsi is proud to announce it has joined in partnership with Tacorama to market the release and conduct fast-food tie-ins. "This is going to be a great taco picture," says Schnapper.

Helming the project will be Joel Charman, director of the romantic comedies *Talking Backwards* and *Final Four*. Taking on his first major action film, Charman is excited for the opportunity to explore a new genre. "I love dinosaurs and I love glamorous women. This will be my most fabulous film ever," he says.

The script is being rewritten by an all-star team of Hollywood veterans. With Rick Drain overseeing tone and continuity,

William Goldman, Shane Black, Ron Bass, Joan Didion, John Gregory Dunne, and Akiva Goldsman are all participating in the rewrite process to produce a perfect and flawless script.

Appearing as Natasha, *KB*'s heroine, is newcomer Chelsea Starlot. A modern-day Lana Turner, Starlot was discovered personally by Hotatsi's chairman as she was sipping an iced blended-vanilla at the Sunset Plaza Coffee Bean and Tea Leaf. Her radiant beauty and devotion to her craft made her a natural for the part. Says Starlot, "I love this character. She is so hard and yet so vulnerable, just as all modern women feel. I can't wait to get into the role."

Anticipating the enormous excitement already building around the project, Hotatsi has reserved the Los Angeles Memorial Coliseum for a premiere party next June.

CHELSEA

My new apartment is gorgeous. It's about fucking time I had some room to spread out and unwind after being cooped up in that shoe box flop pad. Jerry is taking such good care of me. The waiting list here at the El Royale is four years long, but he made one call to the manager, gave his daughter a development job, and voilà!

On the downside, getting clear is becoming a major pain in the ass. It's impossible to focus on my part when I am being gang banged by childhood traumas every time I shut my eyes. My counselor at the center says we are almost clear and as soon as the first check from the film comes in, they will be able to advance me to the highest level where I don't have to deal with this repressed emotional bullshit any longer. But soon is not fucking good enough while I am trying to play a roll and deal with these idiots on the set who don't even know how to put a star trailer together. The one they gave me was facing dead-on west, perfect to soak up UV's all day long. I went to the director and told him he had fifteen minutes to give me southern exposure or I walked and, incidentally, I wondered how they were going to retract all the fabulous publicity about the new Lana Turner/Pamela Anderson. Five seconds later, the crane pulled up and my trailer now has a lovely southern view. I am finally learning how this business works.

Life here is made a little easier by Whitshit's daily trips to Maxim to pick me up some pick-me-ups. On the first day of rehearsals, I told him, "If you think you are going to hang around the set of *my* film, sexually harassing extras all day without earning your keep, I will have Jerry remove you, feet first, in about two seconds."

Of course he turned completely fucking kiss-assy on me. He knows who's running the show now. "*Ba-bie.* Let me know what kind of sugar I can provide to help the bad old medicine go down. You want to park at your trailer and let me help you feel better?"

"Shithead!" I said, "If you ever think of putting your polluted body in the same zip code as mine, I promise that your parents won't find enough pieces of you to bury."

And with that little negotiation, Eric Whitfield became my personal Dr. Feelgood, running frequent trips to Westwood and beyond, keeping his leading lady feeling perky.

Joel, our director, is a clueless, preening clown. In the read-through the only guidance he gave us was, "Be fabulous everybody." Throughout the whole thing, he just giggled to himself and when it was over he got up and said, "I love you all. You were perfect. And I am due at the Beverly Hot Springs for my wrap in fifteen minutes." And he walked out.

So, as usual, I am stuck doing everything myself. The rewrites are complete shit. They have these scenes where Natasha crawls through mud for five miles. I don't think audiences are paying to see me covered in mud. There is no explanation of why Natasha needs danger, why she needs this cute little dinosaur in her life, no real chance to get to know her and for me to display the kind of depth that a real actress can bring to a role. I talked to some of the writers, but each one told me that emotional depth wasn't in their contract. This one says he just does chases, another one only does the dinosaur's dialogue, another one just handles the sex scenes, and another one I spoke to is working full-time just to add pop-culture references. So it looks like I've got to pull two shifts, one as actress and another as writer to put in depth myself. Before we're done, I'll probably have to direct this thing too.

Oh, shit. I am coming down hard and Whitfield is an hour late getting back with a new supply, including my Vicaden parachute so I can get focused and get back on set. Jesus, this is completely fucking lame. How do they expect me to work like this? Well, fuck it. I am not going out there again today. I'll just stay in this trailer until things feel all right again. Morton says there is no higher obligation than my mood. But, damn it. It's no good in here either. They've got the whole place bugged. I can feel them watching me; right now they're all looking at me, figuring out how to sell Chelsea to the world. I could swear I've seen that first AD before. How the fuck did he know my name? Another FBI mole, keeping tabs on me.

No fucking way I'm going back out there. We can shoot tomorrow. If I feel like it.

KILIMANJARO
Big Kahuna Whitfield

If I had known that producing a feature film would be such labor, I would have taken Maxim's advice and become a DJ long ago. Mac Daddy Eric J. is on top now, but this is no cakewalk to the box office.

As befits my top-dog status, I now host a permanent movable feast, beginning every evening in a large corner table at the Grand Havana Club where I conduct my official business. I set up shop at 9:00 and open by receiving a string of writers who pitch me their latest. Word has gotten out that after what I did for my boy Stuey, Kilimanjaro is the must-see, one-stop-shopping production house for all your breaking-into-the-biz needs. I schedule six writers for the 9:00–10:00 spot; each gives me five-minute pitches and then I take five to give them my notes then send 'em home to work. I've sat through two months of pitches and haven't heard anything that sounds like Kilimanjaro material yet. I've put the word out that Dickens is hot and I'm looking for a boy that can give me a modern *Clueless* spin on Oliver, without the music. Maybe set it in space. Do an *Event Horizon* or *Stargate* on it.

At 10:00 my posse assembles: Faisal, Maxim, and some of the Persian delegation, along with a sample of the hottest up-and-coming agents and execs in town. Invited Hirtley last night, but he sent his assistant Wadsworth in his place. The clown took notes through the whole night and kept asking everyone, "Tell me, between us, what do you really think of Todd? Do you think he should get married?" I gotta warn my man to watch his back for this boy. Once the crew assembles, we sample some of the finest Cohibas and Cubanos that I require my writers to bring as the price of the meeting. Had a chance to slip a box to Arnold last week. Gotta ask him how he liked them.

With my posse in tow, we adjourn from the Grand to Bud's, where the Whitfield clout is such that the VIP room has become my personal office. I hold court in a dark back corner like Don Corleone, watching the monitor to see who is waiting at the ropes and radioing word to send the finies back to join me and ma boys. The Whitfield room has become the hottest E ticket in town and Bud lets me have the run of the place, knowing I bring him the best.

However, success does not come without a major price tag. My days are spent on the *KB* set, working double-time to keep my entourage's needs satisfied. With shooting to begin in two weeks, my work is endless. Faisal's cousin's girlfriend wants a walk-on. Got to spend half the day checking out the new talent to ensure the Whitfield suite at Bud's has some hot new party favors in store that night. It's all work getting crew jobs, jackets and hats for everyone's friends from back home.

On top of all else, I am keeping the major talent, my discovery Chelsea, happy with a continuous supply of nose and mouth candies to stabilize whatever psycho freak breakdown she hits in her average workday. I knew that girl had something when I spotted her there at the Bean, and she sure is not forgetting that it is Eric Whitfield who extended the silver platter from which she snatched her stardom. At least I think she's not forgetting that, but she's been a little too busy getting down with her issues lately to express her appreciation. All the same, when the *Break* opens and word gets out that I've been in the saddle with her since before her pony left the ranch, you know every hottie in this town is going to want to take a ride with Eric J., hoping to grab the Chelsea Starlot brass ring to fame and fortune.

What with this hecticness, I haven't gotten over to the Beverly Center to update my wardrobe in two months. Word is that my silver-plated cow belt collection is very quickly becoming old school. But membership in the Big Kahuna Club has its privileges. I do a drop-by on the costume designer, invite her to my room at Bud's, and let her know her job description has just grown. "From here on," I tell her, "you are going to be designing the phat outfits for me."

"Well, what do you want to wear?" she asks.

"Simple," I say, "dress me like a producer."

DEANA

Can I just tell you guys how much it does not pay to have friends outside of Hollywood? People in the hinterlands do not understand what we go through and are not willing to make the tiniest little sacrifices for us.

That is why, if you were wondering, I was in absentia from our weekly get-together at Newsroom last Wednesday. Despite the fact that the script I have nursed from its infancy is going into production, I am now in Westport, Connecticut serving as bridesmaid to my three closest childhood friends. At least I am a VP now and have the power to call up the office and put this conference call together at a moment's notice, because I don't know if I could have made it through this weekend without talking to you guys.

Why, you ask, did I go? How could I risk all I have worked for by running across the country during one of the most important months of my career? Well, let me give you a little backstory.

At the beginning of last year, Becky, Rachel, and Liz—my three oldest friends—from Westport simultaneously announce they are engaged. A more suspicious mind than I might have suspected that their announcements were timed in response to the rumors about my skyrocketing career and glamorous life in Hollywood and that were just trying to get one up on me. Like I say, a more suspicious mind might have thought, but I know these guys better than that. They are just losers who stayed in the East, working in businesses that no one could care less about (Becky is an editor for Simon Someone, Rachel works for a bank! And Liz is getting a—listen to this—Ph.D. in anthropology. How's that for an A-list profession?) Anyway, so they hit twenty-five, halfway to thirty and have nothing to show for their four years out of college, so what choice do they have but to get married? No, honestly, I swear I don't take it personally, I just feel sorry for them.

So they are all making plans and of course they all ask me to be their maid of honor ("But you're the only one we know who isn't getting married yet . . ." they say). And they were all planning their weddings dispersed across the year and I'm just like, "Look, I am totally psyched for you guys finding people to marry you, but if you want me you've got one trip to divide between you, so figure it out." I tell them I will come to Westport from January 6 through the ninth and that is to be my only visit this year. I thought that would get rid of at least two of them. But no, the three bitches teamed up and planned this medieval torture weekend where I've got to be maid of honor three times in three days, wearing a more ridiculous, hip-accentuating dress each time.

Of course when *Kennel Break* came up I tried to get out of it and explain to them that I could not get away from my desk for five minutes even to be Sherry Lansing's maid of honor. But they called up my parents crying and then my parents call me and start in on, "Deana, we're a little concerned that California might be having a negative effect on you." And *violà!* here I am for Always a Bridesmaid Weekend.

Actually, the weddings haven't been too bad. I'm finished with the first two and number three starts in a half hour. The champagne has been flowing and I have been floating on it since I landed. My toasts have gone really well. At Becky's wedding I said, "Looking around the room and seeing all my old friends and family, I want everyone to know that although I may be a vice president at a major studio, there will always be a little bit of Westport inside me. Although I might spend my days now supervising multimillion-dollar productions and developing entertainment products that inspire the entire world, there is still nothing more important to me than standing by the side of an old and dear friend as she walks down the aisle." Pretty good, huh? Rick Drain wrote it for me. I think I'm going to use it again tonight.

I must say, some of the groomsmen are pretty cute. At Rachel's wedding this investment banker from the city was best man. He was completely sloshed and while we were dancing, of course he started coming on to me. He whispered in my ear that he has slept with every maid of honor at every wedding he has been best man at.

And I'm like, "So what do you get, like a banking stud medal for that?"

And then he tells me, "I'd love to go out back and lick your toes."

"Gag me."

But he keeps going: "At work they call me Mr. Bull Market. Want to know why?"

And I just say, "Whoa! Way too much information!" And I remind him that I have a boyfriend, showing him again the copy of Todd's promotion announcement from *Variety*.

"So if your boyfriend loves you so much, where is he this weekend?" Bank Stud asks.

"He has more important things to do than be at some stupid Westport wedding with no one. Besides, we don't have that kind of relationship."

Now he's totally grinning at me. "What kind of relationship do you have?" he asks.

I glare at him for a second while trying to come up with an answer to that one. Finally I just say, "If I let you take me back to your room, do you promise you will not say one more word for the rest of the night? Like if I hear your voice, I am out of there."

He nods and we take off right as they are cutting the cake. Of course, he's done before I even realize we're doing it, and then passes out. So I'm lying in bed with banking dude, my fuchsia bridesmaid's gown in wrinkles on the floor with the bows scattered all around the room, thinking about Todd, about how he must be all alone right now, missing me but afraid to admit it to himself. I just want to let him know it is okay to love me.

And I'm thinking about Rachel and Becky and Liz, about how happy they looked in their ridiculous small-town way. About how easy it is to be happy when you don't have goals and things you want to accomplish for yourself. But still, it did look nice, having a guy in a tuxedo there for you. Being up on stage. Everyone there to see you. Not having to date anymore. I think I will have a talk with Todd.

That is how my weekend has gone. What about you guys? Oh, shit! I'm totally dying to hear what you've been up to but I just looked at my watch and wedding number three started twenty minutes ago. Fuck.

I love you guys. Call ya when I get back.

PULP BLUMINVITZ 3000

I can see now why so many established writers complain about life in Hollywood. For years I thought it was just the big shots, whining about forgetting where they came from and how they got here. But I must say now that I have had a taste of success, those guys have a point. It is lonely at the top.

The boys think I've sold out. When I returned from Mexico, I threw a dinner at El Coyote to celebrate the script sale. Josh, Joel, Jason and a few others of the Reed Mafia were there. I was in a great mood and anxious to share my success with the gang, but instead of excitement, all I got was the silent treatment. No one spoke to me and they just grunted in reply to everything I said.

Finally, I could take no more and asked what was eating them. Joel spoke up. "You're not one us anymore, Stu. You no longer share our principles. Hollywood has changed you."

I was flabbergasted. This from my oldest friends. "Boys," I

explained. "Just because I've made it doesn't mean I'm not one of you. Wait and see. Now that I've got my foot in the door, I'll be setting up the kinds of projects we always talked about. Real gritty over-the-top action films packed with biting social satire. And you'll all be on board. Just wait, guys."

They stared at the table. "You're writing a dinosaur movie, Stu," whined Josh.

"And if that weren't enough," Jason chimed in, "you missed the festival this weekend?"

"What festival?" I asked.

They all chortled. "What festival? Did you forget that last weekend was the annual Korean kickboxing cinema marathon at the Four Star?"

"Guys," I pleaded, "I was in Mexico. There was nothing I could do."

They just shook their heads. "The old Stu wouldn't have let anything stand between him and that festival."

At this point the Pit Bull, who was on his fourth double-margarita on the rocks, entered the fray. "Why you ungrateful bastards. After all Stu has done for you, the first time he gets to spread his wings you turn into a bunch of jealous little high school girls. With friends like these, who needs producers?" And with that, the Pit Bull pushed the table over, threw his head back, and laughed as the margaritas tumbled into their laps.

"Let's get out of here, Stuey," he said. "We'll find us some high-class folks to pal around with. People who get happy for their friends." And we left. Thank God for the Pit Bull, the one man who has stood by me through thick and thin.

However, things were not quite rosy on the other end of town either. I learned that the studio had hired a whole team of writers to "polish" up my work. In fact, I saw a copy of *Variety* at my shrink's office that said they were doing a "page-one rewrite." I called Mr. Whitfield to complain but he reassured me that the rewrite was no reflection upon my work.

"Homefresh," he said. "You are being rewritten by the best. Eyeball that list, the primo scribes del mundo boy-o. You recognize what an honor that is?" He had a point. Just having Rick Drain look at my work, even if he was crossing it all out, is quite a step up from the old days.

Mr. Whitfield wanted to show me I was appreciated and offered to give me a tour of the set. That was really nice of him, considering my work on the film seems to be pretty much done. I think he's eager to work with me again. He asked me to think up some ideas for a modern adaptation of *Ben-Hur* set in women's prison to pitch him during the tour.

When I got to Hotatsi I strolled right through the front gate, just like I predicted I someday would the day they threw me out feet first. I met Mr. Whitfield in his office, a really nice one overlooking the lot. He claims it was where Darryl Zanuck cast *Casablanca*.

Pointing at the sofa, Mr. Whitfield said in awe, "That, mah boy, is the original casting couch. Where they invented the term." Pretty impressive, I must admit.

The set looked great. It was incredible seeing my words fleshed out across a ten-acre soundstage, although I don't recall writing any scenes set on a space station. But if that is the direction they needed to take, who am I to argue?

And then I saw her. Together again, so far away from our night together at the Formosa, back when we were two struggling dreamers—Chelsea preparing her lines cross-legged on the floor, her eyes closed, humming to herself. I couldn't resist the dramatic gesture and snuck up behind her, put my hands over her eyes, and said, "Didn't I tell you I'd get us here?"

She seemed startled and said, "Holy fuck! I know that voice!" When she spun around, something strange happened. I guess now that she's becoming a big star, thanks to my script, a lot of people must stalk her because she seemed to be scared, as though she were confusing me with someone else.

When she looked at me, she let out a bloodcurdling scream that made the entire crew stop in their tracks and glance over. "*Aieeeehhh!* It's him! How the fuck did he sneak in here? Get him out of here! Oh, my God, forget about shooting today! Security!" And once again, I am dragged off the lot, trying to explain who I am. I looked around for Mr. Whitfield to clear things up, but in all the confusion he had disappeared. The security guard recognized me from that incident with Deana Cohen and said that if he caught me near the lot again he would break my legs.

I'll get this cleared up. But anyway, I saw the set of my first major motion picture. And what's more, just in the nick of time, with rent five days overdue, my payday has arrived. I am holding in my hands an envelope from the Neutron Agency containing my share of the profits from the sale of *Kennel Break*.

There must be some mistake. Let me see here, they've taken out 50 percent for Mr. Whitfield, 10 percent for Neutron, 2½ percent for lawyers, 2 percent for accountants, 2500 dollars plus 1½ percent for the Writers Guild, and 30 percent for taxes; 9,433 dollars for Neutron expenses, 2,892 dollars for lawyers' expenses and I am left with. . . . 872.18 dollars. This can't be right. This is a huge movie. Oh, my God, I owe so much money. Let me call Todd and straighten this out. I'm sure there's a mistake, somewhere. This can't be right. . . .

THE NEUTRON AGENCY
Memo: # 14502

I guess I'm going to have to call you Agent Asswipe now, eh? I said I'd get you on a desk, didn't I? Now you see that no force in the universe can stop the power of Hirtley. Even my leftover garbage is elevated to stardom on the strength of my mere signator of approval.

You are now in a position to be doubly useful to me, butt pirate. You will function as my eyes and ears at the junior-agent level. I want a daily written report submitted to me detailing each and every mention of my name within these walls. When you are at the top, there's always a hill full of gooks gunning for you and I need you to scout the trenches and tell me where the bullets are coming from.

Yes! You still have to keep my log. You think I trust that little twerp they assigned me? You think I want her hearing our confidential strategies? Find out everything you can on her. Background. Friends. Apartment. Gym. The works.

Okay, what've we got.

ITEM: Chelsea has gone from prima donna to Pollo Loco. *Kennel Break* is losing two days a week of shooting to accommodate her tantrums and walkouts. She is coked and doped up to her eyeballs thanks to Eric Fuckface Whitfield. Anyone on the crew who tries to talk sense to her is immediately fired by Jerry. So they come to me, her agent, to get her in line. And when I try to talk to her she gives me the hand and says, "You are interfering with my spiritual development." And then she hands me a load of shit about the air on the soundstage being poisoned with negative ions and wanting a special filter for the ventilation system that, incidentally, can only be purchased from one very exclusive church for the low, low price of 1.5 mil.

That tart is headed for no good, shit boy, and if she goes up in flames, she could take me down with her. Not good to be associated with a drug-cult-related-on-set-breakdown, especially when you have cultivated a party boy image as assiduously as I have. A Chelsea disaster following so closely on the heals of Karl Salami's crash and burn would raise serious questions about my long-term viability. It is time to give myself a makeover, a complete image overhaul.

Still, they say Chelsea looks incredible in the dailies. As I predicted, she has the magic.

ITEM: My new so-called assistant put Blumincrap through to me yesterday. The little slob was whining that his paycheck was too small. Amazing how quick it goes to their heads. He is an embarrassment. I want this agency disassociated from him at once. Do it quietly. Better still, you rep him. Keep a lid on him, under wraps, etc.

ITEM: Deana Cohen. Is she that bad? You've got to admit she's a player. On the fast track toward production chief. You look surprised, butthole. No, you are right. This is a change in the Hirtley posture, but life at the top has a way of opening one's horizons. On the strength of my hard-driving party boy up-and-comer status I have now worked my way to the exclusive upper echelons of agentdom. I am now certifiably the best there is.

But I must consider the long haul. What lies before us? Head of the entire agency? Studio chief? Brokering foreign investments? The world is mine if I play my cards right. And that requires softening the hard edges. Settling down, showing potential supporters that I am a stable entity, ready to go all ten rounds, distancing myself from my fellow members of the Neutron party boy Wolf Pack. And besides, as you well know, people are talking. All eyes are on Todd Hirtley and I don't have to tell you what they are whispering. And I don't have to tell you it's not true.

Do I? Good.

Deana Cohen is a power player, not unlike myself. Not willing to let the needs of family stand in the way of a career. Uniting with an exec instead of going the actress route will demonstrate true love and affection, emotional depth. Besides, you have to admit she has lost a ton of weight. Forty-three pounds, she says.

Shitboy, you are witnessing history. My mind is made up.

I am going to marry Deana Cohen. Get her on the phone and tell her to be here at 4:00 so we can call *Variety* together. Push my 5:00 back to 5:30. An event this big needs time to breathe.

JERRY

Hello again you worthless, no-good son of a bitch. One year I spend talking into you and my anger gets nothing but bigger. And one day with Chelsea in front of the play station on the giant screen and I am as happy and confident as a high school quarterback picking his prom date. I'm just checking in to let you know I am finished talking into you. And finished with Dr. Birnbaum, for that matter. I am cured. A new man. And without any goddamn psychobabble. All it took was firing my entire VP staff, starting off a giant production, and a few hours away from the office to relax. So fuck you! You hear that? I said, fuck you! What do you say to that, huh? Huh, cat got your—Oh, right. Fuck it.

Anyway, life could not be better. Between shake-ups and *Kennel Break*, the Hotatsi stock has gained back almost a quarter of what it lost the last three years and the Japs are off my back, happy again. Had a look at the sets and the whole damn thing looks terrific, outer space and shoot-'em-up and thrown in the whole kitchen sink. The word on Chelsea's dailies is she is going to be the biggest fucking thing since Julia Roberts. I've still got the touch, still know how to pick 'em. That director better get off her fucking case soon though or we are going to have to change captains in midstream. Who cares, though? The whole studio is what's is making this movie a smash. Nitwit director is just a cog in the machine.

Okay. Better send an update to Tokyo. Let them hear more good news. *Cheryl!* Bring your pad. Take a memo.

Dear Mr. Morahitsu,

I just wanted to say thank you again for the wonderful vote of confidence you gave me at the board meeting last week. I think I am safe in saying that you have got the right man to pull this studio out of the gutter and your confidence will be justified. You remain a giant visionary in the corporate world and deserve all the success we can bring you.

Update on *Kennel Break* production: We are now into week seven of shooting. Although it is true, as you have probably read, that we are running five weeks behind schedule, this is a standard adjustment that is typically made at the beginning of an enormous endeavor such as this and you will find these numbers reflected in the gross corporate, cross tab referenced, fiscal, fiduciary, master overhead etc., etc. *Cheryl, get one of the Harvard boys to throw in some numbers gobbledygook there.*

Yes, it is true that due to the delay, we are likely to miss our July 4th weekend opening and thus will have to forfeit our deposit on the Coliseum, but this setback is only to ensure that we will bring to the screen the highest quality entertainment the world has ever seen. What is more, our distribution people see an opening in the late August period, when there is a two-week window in which no major-event picture is scheduled to release. With the weekend to ourselves, the film should open at 75 million dollars and repeat that business the following weekend, earning back our projected budget within ten days, *blah, blah, blah. Give him more of that.*

Everyone here is hard at work on the *Kennel Break* project. The toy people have put together a great line of dolls and action figures. The CD-ROM should be the biggest seller ever. The soundtrack will feature new songs by the fifteen of the world's top bands. Across the board, *Kennel Break* will bring billions to the Hotatsi Corporation.

Everyone here looks forward to seeing you at the premiere and asked me to let you know how hard we are all busting our asses for you.

My love to the wife and kids.

> With great regard,
> Jerrysan

Sounds good, doesn't it? Yes, it is great to be back on top. What the—? Why is this thing on? Who's been playing with my Dictaphone?

Nine

DEANA

I know I've said that I was busy before but I had literally no idea
what *busy* meant until I tried to simultaneously coordinate the
rewrite of a major summer release as well as the biggest wedding the industry has ever seen. I am so going to rely on you
guys. I think that for the first time I am understanding what a
support group means now that I have all this shit to get off my
chest. Aren't you guys amazed that in just three months I am
going to be *Mrs.* Deana Cohen, married to the cutest, hottest
up-and-coming agent there is? I'm sorry, make that Mrs. *Vice
President* Deana Cohen. Let's not forget that I am bringing
something to the table here too.

The wedding plans are coming along *magnifique*, thank you
very much. My parents wanted me to tie the knot in Westport,
but I totally put down my foot on that little scheme. I was like,
"Mom and Dad, I love my old friends, but most of them don't
even know what an honor it is for them to be in a room with
Todd. I mean seriously, when I was home, they were like completely in the dark about how powerful literary agents are in this
town. Do you guys really think it's appropriate for me to share
this day with people who can't appreciate its full meaning?"
They understood and totally agreed it should be out here.

Most incredible of all, guess where the ceremony will be? At the *Kennel Break* premiere party! Yes, way! The party's not going to be at the Coliseum any more, but it will still be huge. I got the idea when I read that story in *Variety* about how Ben at TriWorld proposed to Julie from New Horizon on the red carpet in front of his premiere. That stunt got so much play in the trades that I figured that if Ben gets that much heat from a proposal, we'll get ten times that much coverage for a wedding. Besides which, Todd and I are way, way bigger than those guys.

So I marched into Jerry's office and gave him the idea. At first he was totally against it and told me to leave, but when I suggested that it would help the film's promotion to play up a behind-the-scenes love story, he said "Awww, whatthechrist. Just get it over with before the buffet opens." He's such a sweetheart these days.

So when is the premiere? Well, *that* is the big question. Production is running a couple of months behind. We needed some major, like, page-zero rewriting. The original draft Whitfield brought us was totally out of touch with our summer demo, and then we had to start shooting early, before the script was done, to make the summer release. But now that it looks like we are going to miss August, we are adding more adult material that will play huge in the fall.

Jerry is going all-out to make this film perfect and has brought in eight of the biggest name writers to add the adult material. My job is to work with Rick Drain and oversee the structure side. These rewriters get so excited with their funny little ideas that they forget little things like, for instance, the midact climax. Duh! If I wasn't looking over their shoulders constantly saying, "Where's the character's arc here?" and inserting the backstory for every new element, this thing would turn into, like, an art film overnight.

From what I've seen of the dailies so far, the film looks great. Structurally, the script still holds together really well, and that is going to be so important to adult audiences. Although our lead actress is, I gotta admit, fucking gorgeous on screen, she is coming completely unglued on the set. Poor Todd is going nuts trying to get her under control.

Thus, the wedding date is a little up in the air. I'll let you know as soon as the production schedule tightens up and we get a firm release date locked in. You guys are all totally going to be my bridesmaids. I'm so lucky to have so many friends who are still single. It's so rare these days.

No, we're not moving in together yet. We decided with all this work we have right now it would be better to keep our separate spaces. Probably we'll make the move over Christmas if we get some time off. But who knows? I am hearing five pitches today and by Xmas one of them just may be in production with me at the helm.

From the Haus of
KILIMANJARO

Yeah, boy. Big Daddy Whitfield is up to his eyelids in a tub full of hot water at this hour. But don't you all worry your sweet little heads about me. I am going to pull out of this one and come away all squeaky clean and bran' spankin' new! Oh, yeah!

Life on the lot was looking very fine. I got a new angle on the screenwriting process that is so dope I'll be flying to the moon on the next batch of pitches. Check this: What makes for great cinema? Great conflicts. Ya got me? And who has taken the time to catalog all the top drawer conflictos of the world? Scruples, ya know, the board game? The *KB* stylist, who I'm bagging of late, turned me onto the game and it is a gold mine of modern-day dilemmas. So now when I have the writers into the office, I pull up a game card and get: If you saw your best friend's girlfriend cheating on him, would you tell? Would you be best man at his wedding? There's the plot. I tell the writer, set it on a college campus, circa 1977. We call it *Big Groomsman on Campus*, the title that tells the story. Whammo, I have got a six-figure script half written. On my lunch hour I hand the ideas off to my writer boys to pull into fleshed-out script form.

At 2:00 P.M., it is back to the office to do the real work: getting on the phone and securing my VIP room privileges for the night while lining up my posse to run with the Whitfield caravan. Usually I break at 4:00 to receive a visitor from the commissary's starlet corps, who are eager to earn a place on the Whitfield A-list by helping me test-drive the David O. Selznick Memorial Casting Couch. Oh yeah, I am rolling in it, boy. I'm taking care of my *cholitas* though, getting them walk-ons and extra jobs on *KB*.

What's more, I have parlayed my producing credit into master control of the guest list for the premiere. I walked into the PR office, my producing bars hoisted upon my shoulder, and told them I would take the job. They tried to fend me off but I told them, "I wouldn't mess around were I in your shoes. Jerry wants it this way," knowing none of them would have the *cajones* to ask him direct.

Yes, it was all good. The only dark cloud on my horizon was my actual producing duties on *KB*, which consisted of making runs four times a day to Maxim on behalf of Mademoiselle Starlot. The girl was getting out over the edge, boy. Mixing coke and speed with Darvaset and Halcyon and whatever else Maxim threw in a grab bag. And this shit got the babe *reallll* freaky now. She would tell me, "You are so fucking polluted, Whitfield, I want you to wear gloves when you touch my drugs." And she got this idea that I was Beelzbub, planting listening devices in her trailer for the FBI.

This chick's shit would not have flown, but I am telling you boy, on camera, she is amazing. The girl just taps into some demon fire. The crowd in the screening room goes nuts for her dailies.

Because of her in with Jerry and her on-camera genie shit, she's got carte blanche to get crazier and crazier offscreen. Calling me Satan, thinking the entire set is after her, getting the director and half the crew fired. At first she's missing a day a week of shooting to deal with hangovers and crises and by the end of the second month, they have her on set two days a week, tops. They're trying to shoot around her and use the doubles, but production's falling way behind. Hirtley tries to talk some sense into her, but she won't even take his calls. I think Jerry is so far off on planet play station that he doesn't even notice. He sent a memo out to the entire studio announcing that he had made it to the end of *Tomb Raider II* and challenging anyone on the lot to try and beat his score.

Finally, last week, production fell a full four months behind. They're going the adult route, so they decide to smash the whole space station and build a chateau, and Chelsea won't come out of her trailer. Not all day. Not the next day. Not even to take her delivery from Maxim. When Jerry finally notices her missing he calls security to bust in and she's taken crayons and covered the entire trailer, floor to ceiling with bar codes and drawn them all over herself too. As they dragged her off, she's screamed, "You're not going to sell me! I'm not a cereal box!" They've got her now on a Scientology rehab ranch out in the desert for thirty days and production is shut down until she returns.

And now, how my ass gets in the sling. Apparently, Jerry throws a French fry freak out when he finds out about Chelsea and demands a head to roll. A lot of the other *KB* producers have resented the crap out of my privileged role on set and finger me as her drug kingpin.

I'm due in ten with the big boy on my role in the Chelsea debacle. I'm going to give him a page out of *The Godfather*, tell him, keep your friends close, but your enemies closer. That I wasn't helping the gal score the dope. I was watching her, looking out to make sure she got only the primo shit and I've been secretly waiting to report to him. I think I can sell him. C'mon, psyche up! I got da powah and I got da moves, oh yeah!

THE NEUTRON AGENCY
Memo: # 14537

Busy, busy, busy, shitboy. The work of heroes never ceases. The Chelsea situation is causing me some major rectal pain. She was due back on set today, but I just got a call from the Scientologists saying they are keeping her another three weeks. If word gets out that she is sinking this production, we are doomed. She will become uninsurable and my name will be inextricably tied to failure.

The sharks are smelling blood. Did you read that production-gone-awry item in *Variety* today? Hotatsi made a big mistake announcing so early that we are pushing back release date. Gives the vultures the rest of the summer to circle. I can already hear them overhead, squawking, "*Hudson Hawk! Waterworld!*" They forget that *Waterworld* made money in the end. With all of *Kennel Break's* tie-ins and merchandise, it can't actually lose money. Can it?

But facts won't stop them from talking, looking for a victim, and our 10 percent of a potential fifteen million per film star is on the line. Here's the plan: Call over to the studio and have them put me together a reel of Chelsea's best dailies. We are going to sign her for her next two films at discount price right now. Despite what's going on with the rest of the film, the talk on her is still molten. Put out word that she loves her work on *KB* so much, she just wants to keep working right through next summer. Maybe get her in some semi-indy–type shit. Put her in a *Cop Land* now, sign the contract so whatever happens with *KB* she's on her way. Get some artsy gloss to take the sting off potential *Kennel* stink.

But another victim. Hmmmm . . . let's think. What was the name of that limp-dick writer who did the first draft? Bluminvitz? You're repping him now? Perfect. What we're going to do is circulate copies of his original script. Let people see the mess I was handed, show the project was doomed from the start, before Chelsea got on board.

Yes, fuck breath, I know it was me who sold that script, but all the more power to me for what enormous numbers I landed on a piece of shit like that. Leak word to the trades that we are dropping Bluminvitz as a client. This maneuver is right out of Machiavelli, ass monger. He has a chapter where the people are complaining about taxes. So what does the Prince do? Kills his own tax collector, satisfying the people's blood lust, deflecting their attention from the tax issue and confusing the shit out of them while he's at it. So let's give them a victim and make it one of our own. Bring me the head of Stuart Bluminvitz.

The wedding plans are coming very nicely. Brilliant maneuver on Deana's part, throwing it at the premiere. Assures the entire A-list will be in attendance. She is working out well. The engagement has been getting very favorable mentions around town. People are starting to see Todd Hirtley as a serious, grounded player, here for the long haul. I have acquired gravitas.

What do you mean, they're asking why we aren't living together? Don't they know how busy I am? Do they think I have time to move right now? Okay very well. Must make concessions for our public. I want you to call Pac Bell and arrange for my phone to be dual listed under both names. Then anyone who asks for my home phone, we tell them to call 411 and they will hear, "I have a Todd Hirtley *and* Deana Cohen at four eighty-two Spalding." That will get the word out.

As for best man: I haven't been able to get Affleck on the phone. Try calling his office and reminding them that we met at De Luca's party at the Chateau a few months back. He was passed out though, probably forgot. If we can't get him . . . oh hell. Let's have Whitfield take the gig. He'll run my errands like a good little storm trooper and throw the wildest bachelor party ever. Tell him I want the works: cigars, lap dances, hookers, fax machines, everything. Make sure Michael Fleming from *Variety* is there. I'm going to retire my party-boy image with a bang. So to speak.

I hope you're learning, fuckatron. Now get Jerry's nephew on the phone and find out if he's coming over to watch the game tonight.

CHELSEA

It is wonderful to be back at work feeling refreshed, renewed, and 100 percent clear. Everyone on the crew has been so supportive. When I returned, they lined up and applauded my grand entrance. So sweet of them to hold production while I took time to confront my issues. I know I will make it worth their while. Now that my soul and mind are clear, I can put so much more into my performance, give it a power and focus I've never reached before.

I must have seemed a complete prima donna, coming unglued the way I did. But in a funny way, my first taste of success actually brought me to an emotional bottom. When your head is as clouded with demons as mine was, anything good that comes your way will be corrupted by your negative energy. Now that I am clear, I can take success and make something positive out of it. That is what they taught me at the ranch and I really think that they are right.

There were some times at the ranch though when I didn't think I was going to make it. All those sessions with my counselor, pushing deeper and deeper into my childhood, my relationship with my parents and my stepfathers, how I have used others, how I have used sex, what really matters to me. There were times when we would push into the hole in my spirit I would just see darkness and want to say *enough!* I can't look at this. Let me just be passed out under the bar at Coconut Teaser's with a Stoli in one hand and some Persian's platinum card in the other.

But we discovered that image is not the real me. The real Chelsea Starlot is kind, loving, and supportive to the people who can support her and just needs space to be the goddess she is. And that is why she has to succeed and become a film star. So she can have that space to be kind and loving and have an enormous platform from which to lead the world to a new spiritual era based on her power.

Jerry has been great since my return. My trailer was filled with a million stuffed animals and flowers. I think he is a bit confused by the new, loving me. On my first night back he said, "Get yer ass over here. I got the Japs to send me the new Beta test cartridges for the Play Station. I thought we'd give them a test run and call out to Roscoe's for some chicken and waffles."

I told him, "Jerry, darling, I have done much work on myself and I really want to keep things simple and beautiful. Can't we just have a nice, quiet dinner?"

He stammered a bit. "Umm, quiet dinner? Er . . . uh . . . sure. Where?"

"I thought maybe Spago or Chaya."

"What the hell is so quiet about those joints? You want to be surrounded by a bunch of ass-kissing show freaks? And what if my wife is there?"

I sighed, "Darling, I really would just love to see everyone and let them see me again."

He agreed to Spago (I reminded him that he could have pizza but I'm not sure how well he will adjust to the changes I've made. Oh, well; Chelsea has to be willing to let go of things and people that cannot help her any more.

I think the new script is fabulous. I am so happy that there is some adult drama in it so I will really be able to explore the limits of my craft. There was a little, tiny problem though. In one scene there is an incredible speech about the importance of not blowing up the world so that the children can grow up to experience the beauty of love as Natasha does for her dinosaur. It's a lovely piece, but for some reason they gave it to my costar, Chris.

Well, I had a little talk with Rob, the new director. I told him, dripping with sweetness, "I'm sorry, darling, but I seem to have a broken copy of the script. Can you get me a fixed one where my character has the lines that I've circled in red?"

He explained some production problems about continuity and character motivations. I let him wind down, then summoned all my intensity, looked him in the eyes, and said, "In one hour, either my script will be changed or my director will." And I walked serenely away.

And what do you know? Fifteen minutes later a new copy of the script arrived at my trailer. They taught me so much at the ranch. This serenity and power is such a fabulous resource to draw on.

What is this? A note from Deana Someone asking if I will be her maid of honor? Who is—Wait, are they having the wedding at *my* premiere? And Hirtley is involved in this? It's okay. It's okay. Chelsea must not act out of weakness, but out of strength. Chelsea will meditate for fifteen minutes and then let that little shit of an agent know that if his wedding screws up my night, he can count on 10 percent of my foot up his ass.

It is good to be in control again.

BATTLESTAR BLUMINVITZ

My life as a player has just taken a turn from bad to surreal. I am beginning to wonder if I might not have been better off never selling a script in the first place. Sure, I would still be living with my parents in Sherman Oaks, but life seemed so much simpler then. . . .

My rent was due last week but my landlord gave me an extension. I told him about the progress of *Kennel Break* and how I was sure to be seeing more money soon. He was pretty reluctant to cut me any slack. "I read in the trades they're calling it *Howard the Dog*," he said.

"Actually, it's not a dog any more. It's more of a dinosaur," I explained. He gave me another two weeks to pull the rent money together.

I then tried to get Todd Hirtley on the phone to talk about when I might see another check, but after leaving about two hundred messages someone named Wadsworth finally called me back and said, "Mr. Hirtley is no longer handling you. I've been assigned your representation."

A step down, I thought, but finally I have someone really working for me. "Do you know anything about the payroll situation?" I asked.

There was a long silence on the line and then he said. "The agency has decided to no longer retain you as a client. Your papers will be waiting for you with the guard in the lobby."

"What? You are dropping me? Why?"

"I am not at liberty to discuss confidential Neutron business. We strongly advise you not to speak publicly about the Neutron agency or the *Kennel Break* project or we will be forced to take legal action against you. Have a great day." And he hung up. So there I was, cut off from my friends, without an agent, barred from the set of my first film, Mr. Whitfield vanished and rent due in ten days. It was time to get another job.

A long time ago, Josh tipped me off that you can make great money working for the Film Research Corp., the people who run the test screenings for the studios. On the FRC, you get a real insider's first look at the process, besides getting to see the new movies for free. I got a job in the audience recruitment division, basically passing out tickets for screenings on the street.

It wasn't a bad job at first. I was working with a lot of hot and up-and-coming young writers and at lunch break we have a lot of serious film talk. Although it's not quite the Paramount commissary, it's great to be back in heat of things, exchanging ideas with hungry young minds. I got in a pretty heated argument with one of my colleagues who thinks that the Quentin style has become a cliché—as though genius can become trite!

After working a few weeks I was starting to get the hang of it and pull in some real dough. I paid off my rent and was able to take the Pit Bull out for a night on the town, just like the old days. Working out on the streets also gives me a chance to be in touch with real people and not just a lot of Hollywood phonies, and that is very important for a writer.

For every film we screen, we have a different demographic group that we target and hand out tickets to. Sometimes it will be black teenagers and other times middle-class people in their thirties, depending on what the movie's target audience is. One day I get handed two different packs of tickets for the same film; with one pack I have to get eighteen- to twenty-four-year-old males, with the other, women from twenty-eight to thirty-seven. And what do you suppose the movie turns out to be? You guessed it. *Kennel Break*.

After handing out the tickets, I couldn't resist seeing the final version of my work, so I got Andy, my boss, to hook me up with a job tearing tickets at the screening.

They were screening to the two groups side by side at a multiplex in Reseda. After the crowd went in, I stood off to the side and watched all the bigwigs arrive: Mr. Whitfield, Todd Hirtley, and even Jerry himself. Alas, there was not a sign of Chelsea.

I waited until the film started to sneak in but something must have gone wrong with the print. Fifteen minutes into the screening, the crowd was fleeing in droves, running like rats from a sinking ship. I asked one of the fleeing crowd what happened, "Did someone set off a bomb in there?"

"I'll say!" he told me.

Then the bigwigs poured out into the lobby. I overheard Mr. Whitfield telling someone, "It is not a bomb. This Mac Daddy is *the* bomb. A few cuts and this piece is going over for so *mucho dolares,* I'll tell you, boy-o."

On the other end of the lobby, the tone was not quite so optimistic. Jerry and Todd Hirtley were having a major screaming match until Jerry grabbed Todd's tie and started pulling it with all his might. Todd's face was turning blue and he looked like he was about to pass out when suddenly he saw me. He pointed across the lobby and croaked, "There he is. He did this to you, Jerry!"

I was about to go over and say hi, but my boss Andy stepped in and told me to back off. He went to see what the problem was and the short of it is, when he returned he told me I was fired. "I'm really sorry, Stu, but they seem to have it in their heads that somehow you ruined their movie." Oh, well, it was probably time to move on anyway.

I'm looking for another job now. I have a lead on a catering gig that I think will be pretty good money. Rent is coming up again soon.

My phone has been ringing off the hook with reporters from the trades calling me. They ask me bizarre questions like, Why did I insist on total script control of the film? Why did I repackage a gangster script as a family drama? I try to explain how the process worked, but I don't think they are listening.

A story in *Variety* today hinted that my original draft was what doomed the film from the start. But at least I finally got to see my name in the trades. As the Pit Bull says, there is no such thing as bad publicity.

JERRY

Will this town ever cut me one damn break? I must be the unluckiest, most tortured, beaten-up slob ever to set foot in show business. Holy mackerel . . . if I'd have known it would be like this I would have kept my job busing tables in the Fox commissary. Those were the days, I'll tell you. You could take a few minutes to relax after the lunch rush, have a little fun without coming back to work and reading in the trades that you were single-handedly sinking one of the world's largest entertainment conglomerates. Nope, no one accused me of that in the dishwashing days.

Where did I go wrong? I was the viewing public's Santa Claus. I get the two highest-priced directors in the business, the town's ten biggest writers, the entire talent A-list to do walk-ons. Hit every big-money button. Give the picture something for the family. Something for teens. Something for a date. And then I take a few days off, try to get my wits together and I walk back into the biggest shitstorm Hollywood has ever seen.

Did you see the trades today? Everywhere stories about that goddamn press screening. I swear to Almighty that whoever leaked those scorecards is going to find his ass in such a tight ringer. . . . Who could it be? Fuck it, fire the whole publicity department. Worthless bastards couldn't get us out of this story. Can't wait to see the look in their eyes when I tell 'em to hit the bricks. I'll give them six minutes to clear out their desks before security throws them face-first on the pavement. *Ha!* That'll put some fire onto this lot.

No, sir. I am not going down alone. At least the trades got the story straight about how that nitwit writer fucked us royally with that worthless script. Had to write the whole damn thing from scratch—practically myself—for Chrissake. Maybe Dee Dee's wedding will buy us some pity at the premiere. Good romantic story, they'll love that. Jesus and Mary, look at the stock price. It's fallen 4 percent on the Nikkei today and it's not even noon in Tokyo. Do they read the trades in Japan? Oh, my God, Mr. Morahitsu is going to love this. Time to lay low. Go underground.

And fucking Chelsea. What the hell did those lunatics at that ranch do to her? Put some kind of brain sucker in her Perrier and turned her into . . . into a fucking *actress* for Chrissake. Wants me to take her to Paris for *pret*-a-fucking spring collection, can you beat that? Didn't even care that I've been made an assistant instructor at kickboxing class. Well, whatever is up with her, I'll be finding out soon. That boy Whitfield is keeping an eye open for me. Good kid there. Have to throw him a bone one of these days. Set him up with a deal or something.

Okay, Jer, pull it together now. We can still save this thing. Write a memo. We start rewrites and reshoots today. And nobody is going home until this film is fixed. That's right, round-the-clock for everybody from maintenance to legal. Get them to set up cots in the courtyard.

Call the writers back in. Let's give this studio another kick in the pants and save the sinking ship before the baby washes the bathwater down the drain with the kitchen sink. You hear me?

HOTATSI CORPORATION
INTEROFFICE MEMORANDUM
TO: JERRY
FROM: CHAIRMAN MORAHITSU
RE: STATUS REPORT

Jerrysan,

We are very concerned about what you are doing. Very concerned. Bad talk about your movie cost us billions in stock price. You will come to Tokyo at once. Report to the board what is happening. We expect you this week.

We have long enjoyed our relationship with you, Jerrysan. But this is very bad. We cannot lose money forever. Report to Tokyo immediately.

Morahitsu.

RETURN NOTE
Memo undeliverable.
President's office not available.
Return to sender.

THE PIT BULL

Naw, I don't need a lousy attorney. I'm coming clean: I did it all. So you just go ahead and throw me in the clink or whatever you do with political prisoners in this hell-in-a-handbasket town. That's right. I am a political prisoner. Struck a blow for the common man. Whaddya think of that?

My statement? Sure, I'll give you a statement and get it down good 'cause I'm not telling it to youse twice.

It starts with Stuey, my roommate. He's a great kid. Heart-of-gold type, busloads of potential and all that. He's helped me out of a lot of scrapes while the rest of this town would just assume I curl up in a ball and die somewhere. Anyway, great kid. Real talent, too. But when it comes to doing business with these bigwigs and fat cats and studio types, the boy don't got two brains to knock together.

What's this got to do with anything? Everything. I'm getting to the so-called crime. You just pipe down and keep taking notes, flatfoot.

Anyhow, so Stuey's making this movie, wrote the damn zillion-dollar production, and then the second act kicks in. Take the script and screw the writer for all he's worth. That's show bizness for ya. So while they're buying air-conditioned trailers for the director's pet Chihuahua, Stuey's breaking his heinie to pay the rent and can't even get the honchos on the phone. Believe you me, I've played out this tale a thousand times back in my day. But this time it's different. If it were about me, maybe I'd turn a blind eye again. But with Stuey on the line, something's got to be done.

So I decide to call in an old debt and help my boy out. You see, that kid Jerry there; back around '62 or so he was a gopher for the writer's office on the Warner's lot. Used to send him out for sandwiches, that sort of thing. Hardworking kid. So when this producer friend of mine is hiring an assistant, someone to teach the ropes, I sent Jer over, gave him his break, and the rest is you-know-what. Haven't talked to him much since and for sure not lately, but I decide it's time to remind little Jer who his friends are and see what he's gonna do for my pal.

I remembered hearing that Jer'd bought the old Thalberg house and I used to go up there Tuesday nights for cards so I figure I'll do a little drop-by. Grab myself a bottle of Wild Turkey for the trip and catch the bus down Sunset to the bottom of Benedict Canyon. I didn't realize how long a walk it would be (always did it by car in the olden days) so there wasn't too much of the bottle left by the time I got up there. Figured on Jer inviting me in for a nightcap, so I didn't bother to conserve.

I knock on the door and this butler, a real-live butler he's got, comes to the door and asks who is it, givin' me this fish eye like I'd crawled out of the gutter. I say, "Go get yer boss and tell him Pit Bull's here and needs to take a meeting of the minds." I slip Jeeves a buck and tell him to step on it.

He leaves me cooling my heels on the front porch for a half hour until he comes back and sniffs, "Mr. Schnapper is not available for visitors right now. He asks you to leave your card and he will have someone call you back." Well, no one ever accused the Pit Bull of being a man who takes *no* for an answer, especially after I'd practically climbed Mt. Everest to get here, so I told the flunky to step aside and let me in. He starts screaming for help and next thing you know they got this armed rent-a-guard throwing me out on to the street. Some happy reunion.

So there I am, sitting on the sidewalk stewing over this bad hand Stuey got dealt and how their ain't no one in this business who can remember a friend enough for a hi-how-are-ya. And it occurs to me that if ever there were ever a time to strike a blow for justice, this would be it.

I was piecing a plan together when all of a sudden the ingredients appeared before my eyes. Empty bottle in my hand. Limo in the driveway with a full tank of gas. Garden hose. My old handkerchief. I sprang to action, tearing off a notch of the hose. I stuck it in the gas tank and inhaled, making a suction. I filled up the bottle with gas, stuck in my hankie and presto! A Molotov revenge for every suffering writer who ever got off the Greyhound in Hollywood.

I snuck into the backyard, lit the thing up, and let it fly through the living room window. What a beautiful sight seeing all those riches earned on the blood of the working-stiff writer go up in smoke. I stayed out there watching it and laughing myself sick, screaming, "Down with the studio boss! Jerry's head on a pike!" The yard fills up with smoke and family and everyone is screaming and grabbing at me and I see Jerry just sitting on the lawn, crying like a little baby. The guy must be having a bad week. Anyway, that's when the fire engines show up, too late to save the place and you boys enter stage left, snap on the cuffs and haul me down here.

So how do ya like that? You still want to throw me in irons? That is the story of how I struck a blow for Stuey and burned down Jerry's house.

What? Whaddya mean it's not his house? It was his guest house? Youse sure about that? It looked pretty damn big. Well, I'll be.

House. Guest house. The statement is the same. Now where's my phone call? I gotta let Stu know what I've done for him.

Ten

Must keep on target, shitler. Our damage-control mission is flying unsteadily at best. Fingers are pointing and despite all our efforts I see a few of them nudging this way. Now the question is: What are you going to do about it, asswipe?

Yes, the Blumincrantz smear has been exemplary. I saw that *Movieline* did a very snide piece, printing a few pages of the original script. Blumincrantz is taking the fall, no question. But my fear is this: did we get the anti-script line out too early. Have we left them too much time to look up the ladder for bigger victims?

They've got no smoking gun here. We lanced the Blumin boil the moment we saw the threat. And we brought Chelsea on board. That psycho bitch is on-screen fucking magic. Did you see the numbers from the screening. Take a look at this: On a 100 scale—Teenage boys: Film overall: 23. Chelsea Starlot: 97. Number-one problem with the film: Not enough nudity from Starlot. Now look at thirtysomething females. Film overall: 18. Chelsea Starlot: 91. Favorite thing about film: Likable and sympathetic heroine. Un-fucking-believable. Since she's gotten back from the ranch, she's tapped into some Satanic screen presence that she can turn on or off like a spigot. She'll be the next

Pamela Anderson. Or Sharon Stone. Or Kate Winslet— who fucking knows—but she's going to be big and we have got our 10 percent.

It is time to get some paper on her. Send Chelsea a representation contract to signature. Should have done it before, but who fucking knew? I didn't want to get committed if she was going nowhere. She can't walk away from me now, though. I have shown some of her select scenes and leaked her numbers to a few reporters and her talk is phenomenal. Thanks to me, she will come out of this shitstorm unscathed. I've already inked the deals for her next two pictures. Indies for scale to bring her acting bona fides sky high. In one month, she shoots opposite Matthew Modine as the wife of a retarded lifeguard who becomes a world-famous sculptor. Sort of a *Shine* thing. Got *Oscar* written all over it. Not going to make us a dime in commission, but that will come. This girl is our cash cow for the next two decades. Just get me the paper.

Nonetheless, I would call the mood at the bachelor party somber at best. Whitfield rented out Fantasy Island and pulled together some A-list porn stars to give lap dances. Where does he get these connections? Despite the free girls, martinis, and Cohibas, I detected a definite chill. My fellow Wolf Packers gave me the cold shoulder all night. Gould took me aside and said, "If this *Kennel Break* doggie-stink spreads to us, we will trample you into Wilshire Boulevard roadkill." They've been jealous lately. Did I play the success card too hard? Rub it in their faces too much? Find out.

Or could it be Deana? You've got to figure she is going to take a hit for this. She's still a comer though, right? And my new family-man image buys me a bit of sympathy. Christ, what am I saying? She's too damn close. Well, got to stay the course. If I throw her overboard now it will look like I'm panicking. Todd Hirtley does not panic and he does not sweat. Get that message out, fuckbutt.

We'd better cover our bases and cancel dinner with her

tonight. We were supposed to make final wedding arrangements, china patterns, that sort of thing. Why don't you call her
and say that I love her and trust her and think that we'd better
not see each other before the premiere, er, wedding. It's only a
week away. Give her the line about bad luck or something. I
don't care about details. That is your problem. And tell the
switchboard not to put her calls through.

We are getting on top of this wave again. Ride it out with me,
slave. We are one week away from shore and if I crash, it's your
skull my surfboard will dive into.

KILIMANJARO PRODS.

Whoa, baby. How do *you* spell *meltdown*? Can you say the stink
is in so deep that there ain't no laundry detergent in the universe
that's going to get these cats smelling fresh again? But have no
fear, because Uncle Mac Daddy King Pimp Whitfield is going to
take the money and run for high ground before this fireball eats
him alive.

The beauty part is that with all these *grande hombres* slapping each other around to get a piece of this thing, Eric the
Whit got shoved to the sidelines and watched the others eat up
the glory. After that crazy *who-er's* little episode, I worked out a
deal with my boy Jerry to run a special ops mission monitoring
Chelsea around the set. Pretty boring work, as it turned out,
because since she got her cerebellum cleansed, all she really
does off-camera is sit in her trailer and chant along with some
wacky tapes about maintaining her purity. My man, if that girl is
pure, then I am Snow White *and* the Seven Dwarfs. Anyhow, so
I just tailed her around the set and reported back to Jerry. She
didn't seem to mind it much. Every now and then she would
turn to me and say, "Whitfield, why are you such a fetid little
child?"

And I'd tell her back. "Just doin' my job, babe." She made me book half the premiere tickets for her cult buddies, leaving me a *tres* tight juggling act with the remainder.

So they finally finish shooting. PR is in the toilet. They're rushing through postproduction and it is coming out looking like shit. The director goes AWOL after he read the production reports in the trades. So the reins for postproduction passed through the line of succession like a hot potato until they finally landed with the second-unit AD. To cap it off, Chelsea disappeared into the bowels of the cult center. I gave her a ride there after wrapping the final day and asked her when she wanted to be picked up. She turned to me and said, "Whitfield, if we ever cross paths, I don't know you." And she climbed out of the car, into the center, never to be seen or heard from again. Like she's not available for the prerelease publicity tours, can't make arrangements about the premiere. *Nada*. Her section at the screening was filled with a bunch of cult peons wearing sailor suits.

Turns out to be a pretty good strategy, given the way the release is turning out. Somehow, her cult posse managed to get the word out how she was totally uninvolved in the film, playing up the powerless struggling-actress angle and the media are buying it. I read an item in Michael Fleming's column about how the director pushed her around, made her do gratuitous butt shots, and sexually harrassed her. Man, the bitch is going to come out of this thing bigger than the studio itself.

But while she is underground erasing her mind, Big Man Jerry was breathing down my back, calling me every ten minutes to get her over to his *mansione*. When I finally admit to him that I have lost her into the church's bowels, he takes a deep breath and explodes, "If you ever set foot on my lot again, you are going to jail! You here me, *to jail!* I got two words for you, *schmendrick: lifetime ban!*" That was fine by me, because staying off the lot was precisely my plan. I could see the *Hindenberg* falling in flames right onto Señor Jerry's rooftop and wanted to be nowhere close to that bonfire.

I show up at the premiere tonight only because I have signed on as Hirtley's best man. By this time I have parlayed my *KB* producer credit into legend as the biggest party player on the coast, and Hirtley knew here to turn when he wanted to turn out the finies. As I pull up in my black stretch, I can smell blood before I hit the curb. A huge crowd was out watching and cheering as the VIPs walked the red, but the press had its shark teeth blared. As soon as I got on the carpet, Goldstein, an ICBM agent who's on my B list, whispers into my ear, "Welcome to Todd Hirtley's Waterloo. Hope you're not still playing for his team." Goldstein has had it out for Hirtley since he snatched Rick Drain from him three years ago.

Armey Archerd was standing on the dias, announcing and interviewing the stars as they went in, so I decided this might be my one moment in the sun and, what the hell, climbed on up. Armey had just finished interviewing Marisa Tomei when he spotted me walking across the stage toward him. He tried to fake it, saying into the mike, "And here is . . . is . . . a very handsome and talented man, Mr. . . . Mr. . . . ."

I whisper into his ear, "Eric Whitfield. I produced the film."

"The producer of *Kennel Break*, Mr. Eric Nitfeld!" Close enough. The crowd went nuts. The little people love anyone associated with the biz. As I stepped down, I spotted some of the other producers giving me the evil eye, just wishing they had my kind of balls.

I sat in the back of the theater. I don't care what they say; to me, that is one fine picture. Great production values and man, that Chelsea is one hot little piece of action up there on the big. About ten minutes into the pic, the crowd started getting restless. At first, Chelsea's heart-to-heart with the dinosaur had them in stitches. (Was that scene supposed to be funny?) But then when they shoot it out at the preschool, people started fleeing their seats like rats from a sinking ship. I mean, that house emptied. Thirty minutes in, half the crowd was gone.

It was then I saw the disaster fully looming in all its vivid Technicolor and decided to get while the getting was good. I had given up my seat and made for the door when a voice yelled out my name. And there was Hirtley, quivering under a stairwell.

He pulled me into his alcove and says, "Where the fuck are you going, shithead? Have you forgotten you are a member of the wedding party?" The man is freaking.

"Hold on, Mr. H.," I tell him. "I agreed to see you down the aisle, but you didn't tell me it would be through a ring of fire, my man."

"So you're not coming to the party?"

"Todd, my bro-ther. I wouldn't be caught in a mile of that wreck heap now."

The man starts crying on me, actually bawling right there under the stairs. "Whitfield, tell me. Do people like me?"

"Steady, boy. Get a grip now."

"I mean, should I do it? Will getting married change anything? Deana, is she—I mean—do people buy her?"

Homeys, you have not lived until you have seen an agent cry. "Brother, if you got any sense you will get out of here while the getting's not completely screwed. That party is going to be no place for a player to set foot."

He tries to pull himself together and looks me in the eye and says, "Thank you, Whitfield. You'll always be my friend." And I bolt from the lobby like greased lightning.

In front of the theater, I saw Deana running around in her wedding dress, screeching at the ushers, "Where the fuck is he? Where is everyone going? *You're all going to miss the midact climax!*"

She caught me rushing by and yelled out, "*Whitfield! Where the fuck is he?*" But I dove into the stretch before she could nab me.

Homey, I am seriously beat. I think I am going to take Faisal up on his offer and join him for that cruise through the Med on his parents' yacht. He tells me they've got a stacked humidor and access to all of the Sultan's finies. Oh yeah, boy!

BLUMINVITZ REPORT FINAL

My big day finally came. By this point I don't need to say that it didn't exactally come off as I envisioned it. But all the same, I had my first premiere and no one can ever take that away from me.

The day began on a low note with the Pit Bull's arraignment. The judge set his bail at 25,000 dollars, which is a little out of my price range, so it looked like he was going to have to stay locked up until the trial. I tried to use my influence with Jerry, as the writer of his biggest picture ever, to get him to drop the charges, but I couldn't get past his assistant. Pit Bull didn't seem to mind jail, though. He told me, "Stuey, they got some of the greatest fellows you ever met in here. I'd take this crowd over those snooty Hollywood parties any day." He even ran into a friend from the old days who's in on vagrancy charges. In their spare time around the cell block, they've started work on a script. Imagine that, a new Pit Bull opus! I can't wait to read it.

It was kind of lonely having this big apartment to myself. Sure, the Pit Bull could be a handful, but he was the one man in town who always stood by me. I guess you don't realize what you have until it's gone. . . .

After the hearing, I came home to try to get myself on the list for the premiere, but no dice. I called Mr. Whitfield, Todd Hirtley, even Deana, but they were all so busy that I couldn't get through. However, the Bluminvitz luck was still holding. Just as I had given up, I got a call from the catering company that I've been doing some busboy work for, and guess what party they were shorthanded for? That's right: the *Kennel Break* premiere.

I put on my tux uniform (making it look extra nice with my pirate-skull suspenders, in case I ran into Chelsea) and headed over to UCLA. They had reserved the entire football field for the party, expecting a crowd of 20,000 to 30,000. As we set up, Mr. Whitfield dropped in to oversee final preparations. He was pretty surprised to see me and asked what I was doing.

"I'm working." I told him. "I got a job on the catering team."

He looked a little confused but nodded knowingly and said, "Right on, *hombre*. I told you your Big Daddy would set you up, swingin' ya this gig. Now look, my boy, I need some help."

He asked me to make it my personal responsibility to guard ten of the best tables for his posse. I was a little peeved at him for not returning my calls, but agreed. It doesn't pay to burn bridges.

We got the party set up by 9:15 and waited for the crowd that was due at 9:30. Sitting with some of my coworkers, I decided to drop the bombshell on them.

"You know," I said, "this is my movie."

They just snickered and one said, "No, it's my movie. Don't you recognize Kevin Costner when you see him?"

"I'm serious, guys. I wrote the script. *Kennel Break.* It was all my idea."

"From what I've heard, I'd keep that to myself if I were you."

We waited and we waited. At 10:30, no one had arrived. The catering manager called over to the theater and was told it had emptied out half an hour before. I guess the directions to the party weren't clear enough.

Just as we were about to give up, we heard the sound of a man screaming "Help!" and running toward the beverage tent. I saw an overweight, aging executive pant his way toward us. I reached to get him some water, when I noticed the panting old man was none other than Jerry himself.

He rushed inside our tent, grabbed me by the collar, and said, "Don't let him find me. Whatever you do, don't tell them I'm here."

My moment of opportunity had arrived. "Ah, Jerry," I purred. "I've been looking for a moment to chat with you. Thanks so much for stopping by."

"What? What do you want?" he sputtered.

"Oh, nothing much. I'm sure it would be no trouble to hide you. However, there is the little matter of the Pit Bull."

"Who?"

"You recall, of course, the innocent man you are sending to jail for burning down your guest house. If you could find a little time in your busy schedule to grant him a pardon, I'm sure I might be able to help you."

"Anything. Anything, just don't let them find me."

In the distance, we heard voices calling out in the night. "That's them," Jerry said and ducked under the table.

"*Jerry-san! Jerry-san!* We must speak with you!" Eight Japanese men in black suits and briefcases ran through the field. When they came to my tent, the elder of the group stopped and pulled out a copy of *Variety* with a picture of Jerry under the headline, BO BRACES FOR *KB* BELLY FLOP.

"You see this man," he asked me, pointing to Jerry's picture.

"Nope," I answered coolly. "No one here but us waiters and writers." The group harrumphed away.

Jerry came out from under the table and actually hugged me. "Whatever you need," he said.

With the mountains of untouched food going to waste and no crowd in sight, my manager invited the staff to dig into the feast and we had a royal staff party to ourselves.

I decided it was a good night to patch up old feuds and called up Josh from Reed. "What the hell do you want, traitor?" he asked.

I told him I was sorry about our differences and then let him have it with, "I'm at a party. There are mountains of free food and an open bar."

Fourteen minutes later, the Reed crew arrived and we shared a reunion feast, staying up all night and devouring the bounty of my writing career. Jerry even stuck around and hung with us. I think he was afraid to leave and he didn't talk much, just sort of sat at our table crying.

I felt bad for him, but wasn't about to let him out of his promise. At around 3:00 A.M. I asked, "And what about the Pit Bull?"

"Awww, forget about it. Let's go spring him from the joint and sit him down for a nice, quiet drink."

It looked like the beginning of a beautiful friendship.

DEANA

You guys. You guys. You guys. You guys. Can I just tell you for a minute? I am not kidding. My life has turned into, like, *Dante's Peak*, or *Independence Day*, or *The Poseidon Adventure* or some ensemble disaster movie. I am like wigging and for the first time don't know what to do.

Okay. Be calm.

So first of all, the movie is like a historic bomb. I mean, I still think we're going to see huge grosses overseas, but that won't be for a year and the Hotatsi people are milling around the lot looking for victims *now*. Jerry is completely AWOL. He hasn't checked in with the office since the premiere and the Japanese have staked out his house and put a trace on the Lo Jack of his company limo, but he has vanished off the face of the industry. I heard a rumor from Tonya, though, that he was like thrown out of Musso's last night after he and some homeless guy had too many martinis and tried to bust up the place. I think Jerry might have hit Lew Wasserman on the head with a chair.

But like the tragedy of it all is that *Kennel Break* was actually really good and everyone is so small-minded and judgmental that they can't even see that, do you know what I mean? I mean, I stayed on top of that script and despite all the changes, it is structurally so sound you can not find a hole in it. I mean, I mean, I mean, I ran it through all ten of Robert McKee's commandments and every line checks out perfectly. I tell you what I'm going to do. I'm going to find every person in this town who is going around saying that *KB* sucks and challenge them to find a single dangling plotline; just to show me one plot element that is not clearly established in advance; one flaw in the three-act structure, including the mid-act climaxes; one character whose arc does not get tied off; one place where the believability is in doubt. I mean, I swear, it's a really good movie.

Oh, my God, and then my number-two problem: the wedding or lack thereof. I show up with my parents to the stupid fucking premiere and he doesn't even have the decency to have his assistant call and tell me he's having second thoughts. And there I find him, cowering under the stairs, his tux totally rumpled and I say, "Todd, my parents are here. We've got to do this."

And he's just like, "Change of plans, D-shit. No wedding tonight."

And I'm all like, "*Fuck you.* Do you know how much trouble I went through for this?"

And he goes, "Deana, I'm not going out there."

"Do you want me to bring them all in here?" I ask.

And he gives me, "I think it is best that we not be seen together," and he ducks into the men's room.

So naturally my parents are wigging about the premiere disaster and the wedding and they tell me, "Deana, we're really concerned about you. We think it's time you came back to Westport."

Okay, there is like, no way, I am going home. I have worked too hard and given too much to this town to give up now. Goddamn it! Why is this business so unfair? I deserve everything. No one has more earned it or is better at it than me. I'm not going home! But damn it, if I have to go down, I am sure as hell not going down alone. If Todd thinks he can distance himself from me and walk out of this all spic and span and sparkling clean, he has got another thing coming. He practically made me make this movie. That's it. I have got it. First thing tomorrow, I am going to the Neutron Board and filing a sexual-harassment complaint against Todd. I will let them know how he used his position to pressure me into sleeping with him and buying his script. How the whole thing was his idea from the start. Let's see him get out of that one.

Oh, my God, I gotta do it. You guys, can I just tell you, I am not giving up. I am all about fighting for what I deserve, do you know what I mean?

VARIETY BOX OFFICE REPORT
WEEK OF OCTOBER 8-15, 1998

TITLE/	POSITION	LAST WEEK	DAYS IN RELEASE
	WEEKEND BO	CULM BO	PER SCREEN
DEATH WIZARD	1	1	10
	18,953,458	52,643,834	8,563
ME AND MAH SISTERS	2	4	10
	15,634,743	30,627,253	6,953
TIMEBOMB 2	3	2	17
	11,526,627	35,865,815	5,013
WHEEL OF FORTUNE	4	3	17
	9,754,555	28,432,014	4,835
SEE YOU IN HOMEROOM	5	5	24
	5,394,837	25,274,491	2,905
KENNEL BREAK	6	—	3
	2,958,687	2,958,687	1,411

CHELSEA

I have arrived at last. After all these years, I have finally found a place where truly I belong. No more drive-through dinners and counting change for a pack of American Spirits. No more cozying up to bar slime for the next drink. No more secondhand Betsy Johnson. From now on it's Chaya, Spago, and Morton's; life will be nothing but Prada, Gucci, and Barney's. Good-bye bus pass, hello private jet. My new friends from the church just helped me and my assistant pack my crash pad at the El Royale and move into my three-bedroom cottage in the Hollywood Hills. For the first time in my life, I feel absolutely comfortable and content.

Oh, yes, there was that little *Kennel Break* incident. The film did not quite live up to expectations. But my star shone through it all. The reviewers were smart enough to give credit where it was due (remember to have Amy send flowers to that cute little Roger Ebert). The press was on the ball and assigned blame for the fiasco to the appropriate parties. I made a huge hit at the Semels' dinner last night telling stories from the set, poor little lost actress just wanting to practice her craft, manipulated by a bunch of power-mad no-talents. People never get tired of hearing what they want to hear, do you know what I mean?

I've started work on my new film. I just read through the script and loved it. My character is so complex and intense, yet so fragile, I can't wait to get into her. I noticed at the run-through, however, that the director was doting on Modine non-stop, while barely acknowledging his *real* star. Perhaps I'll ring him up and see if he wants to drop in for a nightcap, you know, to discuss the script.

Anyhow, it's dusk and I have to sit on my balcony. I find staring directly into the sunset for fifteen minutes puts me in a very good space. And somehow I just don't feel the need to write in this journal anymore. It's like the anger and rage that fueled my past entries are all gone. Funny how success does that. I think I will burn this notebook tonight. It is time to throw away childish things (and the evidence of them). It's kind of sad, though, in a funny little way, leaving the old life behind. I will miss the old haunts. Good-bye Tin Man. Good-bye Cowardly Lion. Good-bye Limpdick Hirtley. Good-bye Whitsleaze. Good-bye Stalker Stu. But I'll miss you most of all, Jerry, you sweet little man. I hear that the bottom is rubber in Hollywood and the fall doesn't hurt a bit. Be sure to call and let me know when you find out. *Ohhhh,* but I'm unlisted now, so how will you find me? Oh, well.

Ta ta.

Epilogue

From ERIC WHITFIELD

To all my homies in the hood,
    Fear not, my bro-thers. Captain Whitfield is alive and very,
very well. Although the world thinks that my boat sunk down to
the murky depths in the *Kennel Break* shit storm, I am still
cruising in the mile-high club with the apex of Mount Kilimanjaro Productions in sight, oh, yeah.
    Yes, groove on this, homeys. After *KB's* B.O. bow, I thought
it would be a good time to do a bit of laying low. No point stick-
ing your neck out in the middle of a feeding frenzy, if ya dig
me. So I took Faisal up on his invite to cruise on his parents'
yacht. A great chance for me to also do some heavy soul-
searching about my career path, what's important in my life.
You know, to put together a mission statement like that Highly
Effective guy recommends. Deana told me about that book. I
gotta read it.
    We climbed aboard the boat at Brunei and cruised around
the Pacific before crossing Suez into the Med. This boat is
built, my man. Eighteen beds, ten-person crew, satellite dish,
and fully stocked everything just for myself, Faisal and whatever hotties we get our hands on, which is a great many, I tell
you. When we pull into port, the babes stick to us like Krazy

Glue. A lot of them even come abroad and ride with us for a while. I'm getting an eyeful of six gals laying on deck right now.

So here I am, atop my own personal Kilimanjaro, taking stock of what really matters. And I'm on this boat and it occurs to me; I could live like this. I mean, the good life is tailor-made to order for me.

While we're checking out the nightclubs in all the towns where we stop, I'm hearing this hip-hop sound, and seeing how the girls go nuts for it, and I put it together: Why not cut out the middleman of filmmaking and go straight to where the party is, do you dig where I'm groovin'?

So Faisal got his parents to agree to put in a couple of hundred bills to open the hottest, the hugest hip-hop club in the universe. I mean, we are going to make this place the world capital of the rave scene. Between Faisal's encyclopedia knowledge of the music and DJ's, and my Hollywood connections, this bird cannot fail but to fly.

And check this out: With the great publicity from the clubs, we are going to lure all the biggest hip-hop scene stars in as coinvestors to promote the place and then expand to a restaurant chain. Picture Planet Hip-Hop, or the Rave Café. Like Planet Hollywood, but younger and hipper and *hap-pen-ning!* With a dinner rave every night; yeah, boy!

Yeah, brothers, the movie grind was getting me down. All the fun has gone and it's become a business of numbers and egos and work, lots o' work. Becoming a music-restaurant chain impresario is the kind of role where I can get back to the basics: Having fun, throwing a great party, and cruising the hotties.

Well, gotta run now. You're not going to believe this, but we are docked in Tunis and *Kennel Break* opens here tonight. Natch, I called the theater manager and let him know who I was and why I was here. Made it out like I was on the publicity tour. I'm going to speak and sign autographs before the movie, selecting betties to join my entourage afterwards. This will be the first time I've actually seen the entire film. The talk is it's going to be a hit in Tunis. You know, I don't care what Hollywood says, that movie rocks. It's got explosions aplenty and Chelsea shows it all.

I'm off to greet my public. You boys save me a stogie and when I return the party shall commence in earnest.

Yeah, boy. To the top.

TODD

The movers just delivered the last of my personal effects from Neutron. Thanks to the success of my paper-free office, it all fit in one box. Just a few floppies, my Mont Blanc pen set for contract-signing ceremonies, and a picture of myself with Edgar Bronfman taken at the Universal Christmas party last year.

The movers were the first human beings I have spoken to in four days. I have not left the apartment in that time. The phone has not rung. Jerry's nephew hasn't called back. I finished all my food yesterday and haven't gone to get more yet. Not hungry right now.

The little bitch actually did it. She accused me of—can you believe this—sexual harassment. The Wolf Pack have steered a wide berth clear of me since *KB* went south. Jealous and resentful of my enormous success, they were looking to take me down to boost their own pygmied careers. Get me they might, but not one of those turds will ever pack half the firepower that I had in my prime.

Anyway, the backstabbing fucks were looking for a knife and Deana handed them an Uzi. Then they went to my loyal assistant and offered to make him a full agent if he would give them the goods on me. The toad leapt up and turned over a disc containing the diaries I had dictated to him. He'd been waiting for his chance for months. When I get back on top, that boy is victim number one.

I would have had a little clout if I still had Chelsea, but the day after the premiere, one of her cult lackeys picked up her files. She moved over to Duncan Dunn at ICBM. I hear he's a member of her cult. Why didn't I think of that? Why didn't I get the paperwork on that bitch sooner? Damn. Mistakes were made.

So the boys selected— completely out of context— portions of my diaries and E-mailed and faxed them all over town. *Variety* and *The Reporter* both do "inside the mind of an agent" pieces and not one chance is given me to explain what those passages really meant.

Then they convene a secret meeting of the board, with all the old guard present, and pass out the diaries, Deana's charges, the rap on how I've become an embarrassment to the agency, and when I get back from lunch at Mr. Chow's, my office is padlocked and I'm handed orders to clear out. They wasted no time snatching up my client roster either. Drain jumped ship in two seconds flat.

Okay, Hirtley. Pull it together. You've got to snap out of this. You are the best there is. Don't forget it. You were groomed for greatness from birth. We got to the top once and we can get there again. What's Jerry up to? Send him flowers. He won't forget you. Then there's Whitfield. Maybe he's got another script. Find out. Put the team back together.

And then we even the score. First I get Shitboy. Then Deana. Then Chelsea. Then that writer. Then the Wolf Pack. No. No. No. Get the Wolf Pack first. My friends. *Pfft.* Bring them down first.

Okay, we're getting back on track. Got to put a disguise on so I can run out to the market. Perfect. Someone must have left

this gown and heels and wig here. That will do. Get some food,
build up my strength, and start making plans. They will all pay. I
am the best and I will return, or be back.

Exactly.

JERRY

I don't know why the hell I didn't think of this years ago, for
Christ sake. All that time living in fear of this day, and things
couldn't have worked out better. When they finally found me
hiding out in the revolving lounge on the top of the Holiday
Inn Hollywood and dragged me in to see Mr. Morahitsu, I
thought my life was over. You should have seen me; crying like
a baby, begging him not to hurt me. But then my lawyer
showed me the fine print of my deal. To give me the ax, they
had to buy out the remaining four and a half years on my contract—full salary plus benefits, perks, use of the plane, etc.
Not only that, but when they let the word fly that I was out, the
Hotatsi Corp.'s stock—which had plunged during the *Kennel
Break* production—soared to record highs and I was able to
cash in my stock options for more then seven times their initial
value. My lousy accountant tells me that I am now the 183rd
richest man in America. Not bad for an uneducated schmuck
from Queens.

Yes, I'd just like to find everyone involved in *Kennel Break*
and give them a big kiss on the smacker. A shame the new man-
agement has tossed them out on their asses too. Oh, well, let the
new guys try to do better with that sinkhole of a studio.

What with this newfound wealth, I have divorced my wife
and moved into a Bel Air estate of my very own. All the houses
up here have got names, so I've decided to call mine "the Kennel" in honor of the movie that made it all possible.

My contract also included a housekeeping deal on the

lot, with full discretionary funds, offices, staff, the works. So not only am I free of the corporate bozos, but I'm going to get to make movies again, just like the old days. Find a hot script, get some great talent together and just shoot a freaking picture.

I haven't been able to get a hold of that Chelsea broad. I heard that they got a new free-fall ride out at Magic Mountain and I was going to take the chopper to check it out. I guess she's a busy gal now. Best of fucking luck to her. She'll need it.

Well, doctor. I'll be signing off now. I think my anger issues are under control so I won't be needing to talk to you on this Dicktafuck any more. Some of the boys will be over in a few for our poker game. That old buddy, the Pit Bull's coming. We've been palling around again, just like the old days. Oops, there's the doorbell. Gotta run. *Sayonara*, doc.

I said good-bye.

Goooood-byeeee . . .

Doc?

Goddamn it. Which one of you guys knows how to work this stupid fucking Dictaphone. My shrink got cut off—

DEANA

Hi, you guys!

Florence is, I swear, literally the coolest city in the universe. I feel so bad for all of you stuck in Hollywood. Italian food is the best and the men are gorgeous. And yes, I have found one for myself. His name is Marcello and he literally works on the docks, so he is totally buffed out and get this—he actually is into sex, every night. I feel so bad for you guys having to put up with those closet freaks back there. (I didn't mean Patrick, Tonya!)

As you may have guessed, I am not missing Hollywood all that much. Getting out of town has given me great perspective on how fucked up the biz's values are. And Hotatsi is totally doomed without me overseeing development. I mean, seriously, who else on that lot has the first clue about a story? And can you believe that Tonya took my job after they fired me? I always knew she was a complete traitor. Now I want to work in an industry where when you do something that is really important *people appreciate your hard work*! So I have decided that when I get back, I am going to become a social worker. Well, not just any social worker; I mean, more like a manager of social work.

Here's the plan. First, I am moving back to Westport to take it easy while I put together my application for the master of social work program at Columbia. Then in the fall, I'll get a place in the city and Marcello will move to America and live with me. When I graduate from school, I am going to start, like, a social work foundation with grants from corporations and my parents' friends and stuff. So I may be hitting up some of you in a few years to talk to your bosses to help out, if you still aren't making enough to contribute yourselves.

Can I just tell you again how much I do not miss Hollywood? It's so nice being here in a place where people are real, do you know what I mean? You can't understand what they're saying but Italian people like Marcello have this intensity that is, like, totally unmistakable.

Anyway, so what have you heard about Todd? I hear no one's seen him out much lately. Wouldn't it be funny if he just hung himself over me? Oh, God, I shouldn't even joke about that. What if it came true?

Well, got to run. Marcello and I are going to eat. The men in this country like you to eat—a lot—and I aim to please. I think I've put back the freshman fifteen since I've been here. You guys have got to come and visit when I get home. I can't stand to think of you stuck in that town forever.

Ciao.

Love ya all,

Deana

DATELINE: BLUMINVITZ

So after all that fuss, I'm back with the 'rents in Sherman Oaks. I was afraid to resort to this for so long, but it turns out that life here is pretty damn good. I've got cable TV, a refrigerator full of food, a big air-conditioned house to myself during the daytime and best of all, I don't have to work anymore. The Pit Bull is doing all right too. Jerry set him up writing at his new production company, so he's got his own pad and a little cash to buy me meals and take me out on the town. He asked if I wanted to crash on his couch until I get back on my feet, which was really nice, but I know now that he's back on top, the Pit Bull's going to need some room to roam. I can't wait to see it.

I've been hanging with my old crew again, you know, the Reed Mafia. It's great to be back with the boys, staying up nights, barhopping, 4:00 A.M. intellectual jam sessions over bacon and eggs at Swingers. I hate to admit it, but I think they may have been right about my head getting swelled by the *Kennel Break* success. It's scary to think how quick I sold my soul to become a big-time player. Next time, I do it My Way. Meanwhile, I've become something of a celebrity in the up-and-coming circuit. After all, there aren't too many guys who make it big and still remember where they came from. We went to a party in Mankin's backyard and lots of people were asking me for advice, wanting intros to my agent. That was kind of cool, but I don't want to be a star. I'm just going to stay one of the guys.

Jason and I are pounding out a new script. It's a modern-day kung fu action-drama, about a team of small-time hoods that uses martial arts to fight the bigger organized crime circuits. I think this one has the potential to really make my name. I asked Jerry if we could pitch it to him but he told me, "Stu, I love you, but the only thing I ever want to read from you again is your obituary." However, he said he's got a few "so-called friends" who he wants to send special presents to, so he's pulling some strings to set me up with pitch meetings. Oh, well, there are lots of buyers in this town.

I've been trying to get Mr. Whitfield on the phone to talk about my new project, but he seems to be up to new tricks. His answering machine has changed the name of his company from Kilimanjaro Productions to Kilimangrooveoh Party Machine. He called me back and left a message saying, "Film is dead, mah boy. It's all about the mix now." I wonder what that means?

Someone has been crank-calling my line at my parents' house. A man leaves messages in a really bad fake sultry woman's voice saying, "Is the big screenwriter there? Got another hot project for me? What are you wearing, Stuey? You'll be wearing a cement block on your feet at the bottom of the river soon. You want to sleep with me? You'll be sleeping with the fishes." I finally star-69'ed it and got Todd Hirtley's voice mail. Strange.

I think I am finally over Chelsea. Yeah, I've got to say, reading these profiles of her and seeing her on the big screen was a real turnoff. I think she has sold out her artistic integrity and she just no longer seems the struggling young actress I knew. Well, I hope she's happy having to hang out with those snooty wheelers and dealers. God knows, I wasn't.

Who needs Chelsea, though, when I have met a new girl. Well, I have not exactly met her yet. I found her on-line in the Chow Yun-fat chatroom and we've been exchanging E-mail for a month. She's an actress (yes, another one! I guess I'm hooked.) from New York and she actually loved *Kennel Break*. She totally got my spoof of Hollywood filmmaking. She loved it so much, in fact, that I have to go now to fly to New York to meet her. Josh just got here to give me a ride to the airport. Who knows, in six hours I may be with the future Mrs. Bluminvitz. I think she may be the girl to make an honest man of me.

I learned a lot from the *Kennel Break* experience. I know now how to survive with your integrity intact. For all the knocks I've taken, if I had to do it all over again, I wouldn't change a thing.

From *US* Magazine——, 1998
"CHELSEA'S STAR RISING"

"You know," Chelsea Starlot whispers devilishly, peering at me seductively over the rim of her flute of Perrier in United Airline's New York–bound first-class cabin, "sitting up front, I still feel like I'm about to get caught and sent toddling back to coach where I belong. I think I'm a bit of a stowaway."

Looking at Chelsea now, it is hard to imagine that she has ever been anywhere but first class. In her Prada suit and signature runaway blond curls, Starlot has already become *the* icon of high fashion to millions.

Her road to fame and glamour was not always an easy one. Although raised in the aristocratic enclave of Westport, Rhode Island and educated at the famed Swiss finishing school La Roset, Starlot's burning artistic drive led her to cast away her silver spoon and take a drive down the road of hard knocks.

"When I graduated school," she lilts, her European accent peeking through, "Mum and Dad had planned for me to take the grand tour, settle down with some steady corporate man, and begin a long and successful hostessing career. But I needed to experience life and I burned to act."

Striking out on her own, Chelsea took to the life of the struggling actress like a duck to water. *"That,"* she says, "will always be where I feel I belong. I try so hard now to preserve the bohemian bonhomie, the camaraderie, the artistic freedom of those days. Yes, it was a struggle. But it was so much fun."